THE IMPULSIVE HORSE TRADER

MAX PORTER

Printed in the United States of America

THE IMPULSIVE HORSE TRADER

I had come for my twentieth high school reunion and was being pushed into something I didn't want to do. Some clown had brought in a karaoke machine and declared that everyone in the class had to sing a song. My hope was that with so many people in the room they would not get to me before it had lost the interest of the crowd. My name was about fiftyish on the list and I couldn't believe that the crowd would still be enthused about laughing at a bunch of people they really didn't remember, making fools of them self.

As they got closer to my name, I gave a lot of thought to just leaving the building. I was torn between having the folks see that I couldn't sing or see that I was a coward. My name came up before I had made the decision and I was trapped.

I stepped on the stage with my heart pounding. I picked up the mike and said, "if my name was Abbot or Akers and I had to come up early, I wouldn't have had the courage to come up here. But now that I see how bad everyone else sings, I figure what the hell. There are a couple of problems however. I didn't bring my guitar. But since I don't know how to play it, I guess that doesn't matter too much. The second thing is a little more serious. I only know how to sing in the shower, so I'll have to get naked," and I started unbuttoning my shirt. The room erupted with cheers and jeers.

I went right into the song while they were making a lot of noise. I had picked Pledging My Love because it was a simple song and very short. I was glad for the cheers and jeers during the first part when I was nervous and I had hit a groove and found the key by the time they could hear me. I managed to escape without embarrassing myself and vowed to never let myself get put in a spot like this again.

I had almost made it without singing. They only had three singers after me before someone stepped up to the mike and made the announcement that we had to end this program because we were due at Cracker Barrel in a half hour for a turkey and dressing dinner. He cautioned us to not think because we were at a high school reunion, we should act as if we were still in high school. Please no racing on the way over.

I was not sure that Cracker Barrel had enough seating for a group this large. I was worried that it would be a disaster and some people wouldn't have a seat. But it turned out to be perfect. They had moved all of the tables into groups that held ten people at each grouping. It turned out to be more seats than were needed.

The seating was free choice and I noticed that the ones who had brought a wife or husband went out of their way to not sit at a table with someone they had dated in school. It made for a few awkward moments, but all in all it worked out pretty well.

With near two hundred people to serve, it was a painful process even though they had a lot of servers. We had not received any food at our table yet when a lady that I didn't know, asked the table in general, "did you see what Trump said about immigration this morning?"

I said, "hold it folks. The two things that should not be discussed at a gathering like this are religion and politics. If you are going to discuss those things I will move to another table."

She glared at me and said, "we can talk about anything we choose to talk about."

I had no idea who this gal was and don't think I had ever seen her in my life. I said, "I came here to see old classmates and visit with old friends. I have no intention of having a duel of words with someone I don't even know, about something that has no place at this type of gathering."

She was shooting me with a pure evil look now and said, "you are obliviously a Trump man and know you can't defend him."

"I have no intention of defending any politician. They are adults, and if they can't defend themselves, they need to get out of politics."

"Well, that may be true, but my Senator said that after what Trump said this morning, he was going to drive him out of politics in disgrace."

"Who is your Senator?"

After she gave me a name, I said, "I never heard of him. And you know what? I bet he never heard of me. We are even and I would like to keep it that way. But I suspect some unknown Senator will play hell driving any President out of office."

She said, "you sir, are one pompous ass."

A group of servers descended on our table with our dinners. As soon as they finished serving, I finished my little speech. "The reason politics should never be discussed at a gathering like this is because the people who are mentally challenged get mad too easily."

With that barb, I picked up my plate and went to another table. The main reason I left was because she had taken hold of her water glass and I didn't want to wear it. She was one insult away from throwing it on me.

I went to the first table I saw with a seat open and set my plate down. I said, "if this table is not talking politics, I would like to join it."

Someone at the table said, "we were just talking

about the news coverage, and that isn't quite politics, have a seat."

As I settled into the chair I said, "I have something to contribute to that discussion. A lot of years ago Napoleon said, 'that hostile newspapers were more dangerous than a thousand bayonets.' I believe he was right."

That started a lively discussion that near everyone at the table weighed in on. The finale consensus seemed to be that even though the news was slanted different ways by different people, it still had the role of keeping the politicians aware that someone was watching.

My first quote had caused a good debate and I added another quote for discussion. "About twenty years ago a veteran journalist speaking at a conference of journalist, made this statement."

He said, "The irony of the information age is that it has given new respectability to uninformed opinions."

The table went quite while everyone thought about that statement. One of the guys said, "I don't understand what you mean by that."

I turned to his wife and asked, "who is your favorite actor?"

She thought about it for a minute before she said, "I guess I would say Brad Pitt."

 "What if the reunion committee had been able to get Brad Pitt to speak at our dinner? Now let's say that Brad Pitt is a democrat and your Senator is a republican. During Brad's speech, he says that your Senator is a really bad guy and should be drummed out of office. Now because he is Brad Pitt you respect his opinion and say to yourself that you will not vote for the Senator in the next election. The truth might be that Brad has never met the guy and has not checked his voting record and in fact doesn't know anything about him at all, other than he belongs to the other party. This would be a case of you respecting an uninformed opinion."

The entire table came alive on that one and I added one more jab before I walked away. I said, "that statement was made twenty years ago and we all know how digital communication has increased in the last twenty years. A ten-year old kid can now have a blog that he is putting all kinds of miss leading information on. No one has the slightest idea that the information is coming from a ten-year old that is just fooling around. A certain number of people will believe some of it even though it as no basis in fact."

I had finished my meal and as I walked away, I had to smile at the buzz that was going on at the table. Everyone was talking at once and I expected they would still be arguing about it at one or two in the morning.

I saw four guys that I had known pretty well in school all standing in a group talking, and I walked over to visit for a while. They were all complaining about the roads under construction. No matter where you were coming from you ran into construction. One of the guys said that the most irritating thing was that it took so long for them to complete a project.

I couldn't let that pass without a comment. I said, "highway projects take so long because all road contractors use the fifty and two rule." They all looked at me as if I had slipped a gear and I said, "the fifty and two rule says that if a project takes fifty men to complete in two years, you should put two men on it so you can drag it out for fifty years and keep that government money coming in."

They all groaned and one of them said, "only you could think of that. You haven't changed a bit since high school."

I said, "I just wanted to clear up the confusion for you. You need to know how things work."

They all groaned again and turned heading for the parking lot.

We were going back to the basketball stadium for a dance. They had a band and a fully stocked bar. It was decorated very nice. Someone had put a lot of time and effort into this whole reunion. I sat at an empty table and waited for the band to start playing. There was only five of them and they were actually pretty good. They played hit parade songs from our senior year and two of the guys could really sing.

They had been playing about a half hour when an attractive lady approached me. She was familiar but I couldn't place her to a name. She said, "don't sit here like a lump. Come and dance with me."

I said, "you don't want to dance with me. My prom date is still in therapy. But if you sit, I will buy you a drink and dazzle you with my conversation."

She laughed and said, "that's the best offer I've had tonight." She took a seat and said, "I'll have a screw driver."

I went to the bar for her drink and while the bartender was making our drinks, I asked one of my classmates standing at the bar who she was. As soon as he told me her name, I remembered her. I had never dated her in school but I had dated one of her friends for a while.

We had a nice easy conversation. She told me she was divorced with no children and I told her I was divorced with twin daughters. I failed to mention that I was actually divorced more than once. I didn't think she needed to know all of my baggage.

When the band took a break, she went to the lady's room and was gone quite a while. I had decided she wasn't coming back and was thinking about leaving when I saw her walking back. She told me that everyone had decided to use the rest room during the break.

The band returned and played a couple of rock songs to wake everyone up. One of the band members announced that they had a request to play a couple of belly-rubbing songs, and they launched into My Prayer. She jumped up and took my hand and said, "come on, you don't have to know how to dance to this music. You can just close your eyes and stand there and sway."

I didn't have a lot of choice. She had committed me to the dance floor or make a scene. I went to the dance floor and it turned out to not be so bad. They followed the first slow song with another and while we were dancing the second song, she told me that the two girls she was sitting with had bet her lunch tomorrow that she couldn't get me to dance.

I told her, "that I was crushed. I thought that my sex appeal had drawn her like a magnet."

She laughed and said, "it did. That's why I took the bet."

We had a very pleasant evening together, but it was not going beyond that because I lived in California and she lived in New Hampshire. I wasn't in to phone sex and doubted I would be very good at it. This was a perfect example of a one-night stand.

The night was winding down, and they threw me a curve. Someone took the microphone and said. Do you guys remember the Sunday night radio program that Graham Peterson had. He bored us to death with his comments but we listened because he played good music. I think it is right that we close this reunion with a few choice words from Graham. What do you think? Of course, every one started clapping just to be polite. But they kept it up until I went up to the mike.

"First of all, I want to praise the group that put this thing to gather. They did a wonderful job. They put a lot of thought and work into this meeting and it went off without a hitch. Thank you all.

My take on the reunion is that there were not too many surprises. The people that worked hard and actually studied, all seemed to be successful in academics or technical fields. The ones that coasted through school without a care like me, have coasted through life. I have put contentment before ambition and I can say I have thoroughly enjoyed every bit of it." Someone shouted from the back, "but what about your sex life?"

"I can say that my sex life has been top notch. I have had three wives and fifty girlfriends. The fifty girlfriends are the reason I've had three wives. Wives don't like that shit." They started clapping and I waved and went back to my seat.

On the flight home, I was relaxing and had nearly fallen asleep when the lady in the window seat decided to go to the rest room. She apologized for bothering me as I moved to let her out. She had laid the book she was reading in the seat while she was gone. I looked over to see what she was reading and saw that it was Gone With The Wind. When she came back, I asked her if this was the first time she had read it and she told me no. She had read it before but it had been a long time ago. I asked her if she knew anything about Margaret Mitchell. When she said no., I told her that the most interesting thing about her was the way she died.

"Her husband had a massive heart attack and was an invalid for quite some time. He had recovered to the point he could get around a little and they decided to go to a movie. The theater was on the side of a hill and they parked across the street. She was helping him across the street when a car came roaring over the top of the hill. She left her husband in the middle of the street and ran up on the sidewalk. The kid driving the car saw the guy in the middle of the street and swerved to miss him and ran up on the sidewalk and hit her. She died later in the hospital. It shows how life is coming from all directions and is very fragile. She was only forty-eight and left her husband with millions but he only lived another three years. Her brother ended up with the money and one of his sons left it all to the Catholic Church when he died. What a waste of an important fortune."

She went back to reading her book and I fell asleep. I don't think she believed me but it was true.

I arrived in Los Angeles about midnight and was not surprised when my friend was not there to pick me up. He was a great guy but the most unreliable person I have ever met. A lady who has a stable near mine where he used to hang out before he started hanging out at my place, calls him Dudley Do Right because he was always screwing up one way or another. This was going to be a two-hundred-dollar cab ride. I lived way out in the Valley. I gave him another half hour before I decided he wasn't coming for sure and fumed all the way home in a cab.

He is the strangest person I ever met. He bought a horse from me about a year ago and to my knowledge has never had a saddle on him since he has owned him. I guess he bought the horse to have a reason to hang around.

He is a good looking, clean cut guy who looks like money. I guess he comes from money because every time he seems to be in need, he goes to Texas to spend time with granny. When he comes back, he is flush again and buys a new car. Since I have known him, he has had a Lotus and a Porsche.

A few months ago, he came to me with all of the information on a trip to Tahiti. We had made two trips to Hawaii together and he decided that this time we should go to Tahiti. We picked the time and planned to stay a week. The flight leaves at seven o'clock in the morning and I go by myself because he doesn't show up.

The trip turned out ok because I met a girl from Germany. She spoke almost no English and I spoke no German but we managed to communicate and had a fun week. When I came home, he acted like it never happened and never mentioned it.

To give you an example of why I think he is strange I will tell you about one of our Trips to Hawaii. We are staying at the big hotel on Waikiki Beach. The first day we meet a girl from Georgia who is there for some kind of conference for her company. She is a beautiful girl and Dudley is in love. He puts a rush on this lady like you would not believe. Every spare minute that she is not in the conference he is in the bar with her. Every day he tries to take her back to the room and she keeps putting him off. Finally, on the last day she is going to be there she tells him that the wind-up night will be fairly early and she will call him when she gets back to her room.

About eleven o'clock the phone rings and we had just gone to bed. We had a room with two Queen beds and the telephone was on a night stand between the beds. I answered the phone and the sweetest little old Georgia Peach voice said, "Hi, it's Susan. I am in room four twelve. It's directly above your room, come on up."

I said, "honey, you got the wrong guy, hang on a minute."

I handed the phone to Dudley and he listened for a minute before he said, "ok, that's great, I'll be right up." He hangs up the phone and turns over and goes to sleep. He had probably spent five hundred dollars in bar bills hustling this girl for a week and turns over and goes to sleep when she finally says yes.

I was glad to be home. The next morning, I was up and checking things bright and early. I had a stable that I leased from a big development company. It had been a really nice Thoroughbred farm at one time. It had three barns, two houses, and four one-acre paddocks left from the original farm. It even had a race track. The company was holding it for future development and it fit my needs perfectly. I had forty boarders and rented one of the houses. One of the barns had an apartment on one end that held my two Mexican helpers. The house that I lived in was really nice. It had a huge paneled living room with an open beamed ceiling and a stone fireplace as high as my head. On both sides of the fireplace were French doors out to a paved porch-patio. It was a great place to entertain.

It had a couple of things you don't normally see in a house. It had a real working pay telephone on the wall near my desk and it had a sign over the door to the bedroom that read Historic District. Both of those things draw a lot of questions from first time visitors.

My real income was from horse trading. I always had on hand from ten to twenty horses for sale. I had learned the business over a period of twenty years and established myself with a good reputation. I made a comfortable living and had a lot of fun doing it.

Everything was running smooth. My guy that spoke good English told me that a man had come by twice to look at the mare. I had a young well-bred Thoroughbred mare that I had bought in Kentucky at auction. She had just turned five and had great confirmation. I had priced her to him for five thousand dollars and he must be interested if he came by again to look. I really didn't care one way or the other if I sold her or not. Young mares with a good pedigree were like money in the bank. I had paid three thousand for her intending to double my money. The only reason I had priced her for five was because he was a good customer. In the past year I had sold him three mares and expected to sell him more in the future.

The gentleman who was interested in my mare called and offered me four thousand. I told him that I would like to help him out but I couldn't take that for her. I thought she was a bargain at five and I couldn't take less. He asked if I would deliver her and I told him I would. He said he would be at the farm in the morning if I had time to bring her then.

His farm was near the old Reagan ranch out by Thousand Oaks. It wasn't very far of a drive for me and I was there by ten o'clock. He gave me a check and asked if I had ever been to London. I told him that I had and liked it there. He said that he was going tomorrow and coming back the next day and asked if I would like to go along. He was going by himself in the company jet and would like the chance to talk horses. It sounded like an interesting couple of days and I said why not.

I met him at the Burbank airport at seven in the

morning and we were on the way. It was a nice plane and had seating for ten people. I could see why he wanted company. It would have been a lonely trip with just him by himself. We talked about blood lines and breeding nicks. We discussed stud fees and how they arrived at the prices they charged for them. We talked about the prices of yearlings and the expenses of breeding and raising a yearling.

I explained my opinion that it was more economical to buy a yearling than to raise one. If you breed one you take what you get, and they will not all be desirable. If you buy one you can pick only the best. If you were to compare twenty yearlings you raised to twenty you purchased, I am sure you would find the purchased ones were more profitable. This would not be true if you had a large operation that raised a hundred plus every year. The economy of size would swing in favor of raising them, and you would increase the odds of getting the big horse that would pay for everything.

We landed in London and took a taxi to the hotel. We turned down a street that was completely blocked by poster carrying protesters. There were two or three thousand of them. The cab driver explained that the Muslims were protesting. He said they are always protesting over something.

The cab driver spent the next half hour complaining about all of the immigrants flooding into the country. His complaint was that they had left their country because their culture had broken down and wasn't working. Then they come here and try to bring their culture with them. He said that not a day goes by that at least one of them doesn't try to tell him how much better their culture is. If it is better, why in the hell don't they stay in it. I could tell he was passionate about this and I didn't say a word. I was glad when we reached the hotel because he was working himself into a rage. I was afraid he might go back and run over some of the protesters. I was glad when he dropped us at the hotel.

We went to a pub and had fish and chips for diner. I have never understood why Americans cannot duplicate The English fish and chips. There, fish and chips are delicious and at home, they are so-so and tend to morph into a soggy greasy mess.

My host told me that he had a meeting at eight o'clock and it should take no more than an hour or two. We could fly home as soon as he was finished. I went down to the restaurant and had steak and eggs for breakfast. He was correct in his estimate and was back before noon.

On the way home he seemed a lot more relaxed than he had been going. We talked about horses most of the time and he was the type of guy who listened to what you had to say. He was smart enough to know what he didn't know. I told him about my library. I have the Blood Horse Stud books going back several years, and I have the Racing Manuals for the past thirty years.

I have books about breeding theories and breeders. I have books about training theories and trainers. The Racing Manuals are great because they list all of the horses that started in the year and all of the trainers and owners. If you are looking for something specific, you can find it on the internet. But if you just browse through the books with no horse or trainer or stud in mind, it's amazing what you find. Before you know it, you have absorbed an amazing amount of knowledge. You could never know it all but you will be ahead of a lot of the breeders you are dealing with. He with the most knowledge has an advantage. That is a good edge to have. I can't tell you how many times I have had breeders give me information about their horses that I know isn't true. Knowledge has probably saved me a lot of money over the years, but I mainly browse because it is fun.

The pilot announced that we were an hour out of Burbank and he finally got around to the reason he had asked me along. He told me that he had bought six hundred acres and was going to enlarge his breeding farm. He wanted to know if I was interested in being his farm manager. I told him that I was flattered, but I didn't have the temperament to be someone's manager. I explained that I had made all of my own decisions for so many years I would chafe under supervision. I buy and sell horses and both ends of that equation are based on impulse. I would describe myself as an impulsive man. In the auction ring you must make your decisions in a matter of seconds, and you buy or pass on impulse. I have in the past bought horses for someone else at auctions and I don't like it. When you are investing you own money there is a certain amount of anxiety that you learn to live with, but when you are investing someone else's money the anxiety level increases be ten. I would not be happy in that position.

He said that he fully understood my point and had no hard feelings on being turned down. He said that he would hire me as a consulate from time to time if that would be alright. I told him that was perfect for me, and I was at his service any time he needed me. He gave me his card but it only had his name Hugh Edward and a phone number. It didn't tell me what company or his position with the company. We landed in Burbank and I thanked him for a nice trip. What a pleasure to fly in a private Jet. If I ever get rich, I will buy one.

The owner of the Los Angeles Horse auction had purchased the auction in Fort Smith Arkansas. He phoned to tell me that a lady who owned a horse farm in Texas had contacted him about having a thoroughbred auction. She had a stud that she was trying to prove and she had purchased a group of well-bred mares and put them in foal to her stallion. She had twenty of these mares that she wanted to auction off so the foals would be spread over a large area and among different trainers. He had declined the request and recommended that she put them in the fall auction in Little Rock for her best results. He thought I would be interested in going to the auction and I certainly am. I see him near every Friday night in his auction in Los Angeles and I appreciated the heads-up call.

I had not seen Dudley since he didn't show up for the flight to Tahiti and I was surprised when he showed up at the stable and acted as if he was just there yesterday. That was the thing about Dudley, it never occurred to him that you might be mad at him. He came to tell me that he was buying a sail boat.

I have never been sailing in my life and didn't understand why he thought I would be interested in a sailboat. He explained that he had found these beautiful little French sailboats at an unbelievable price. It seemed that someone had the idea of becoming an importer of these boats. He had arranged financing from a small private bank in Downey and had bought twenty of them. They were sitting at the dock in Long Beach and he had run out of money already. He had not factored in all of the expenses of renting a place to sell them from and the shipping cost and several other things. He had sold less than a handful before his money had run out. He had just walked away and the bank was now trying to sell them.

He wanted me to go down to the bank where they had one set up in the parking lot, to see it. I was not doing anything in particular and said why not? We drove down to Downey. I have to admit it looked strange to see a sailboat sitting in the middle of the parking lot at a bank. It was kind of an attention getter. What surprised me was how nice the boat was. It was twenty-six feet and all fiberglass so minimum maintenance. They had a ladder attached so you could go aboard and it was really well designed. The cabin had benches on each side that ran the length of the cabin and were wide enough for comfortable bunks. Not being a boatman, I didn't think about some of the things it didn't have, such as a head, and a motor. The price seemed rock bottom cheap to me but I wasn't sure. After we left the bank we drove down to the coast and went to two boat brokers and looked at boats. The boats of the same size and style were twice the price and at one of the dealers three times the price. I had to agree that he was getting a great price on the boat.

A friend of mine was at the barn a couple of days later and we were just sitting around talking. The wind was blowing like hell and it seemed to me that it would be a great day to go sailing. I asked my friend if he had ever been sailing. He said he had never even thought about it. I said they have little sail boats at Westlake to rent. Let's go over and give it a try.

The boats were open and about sixteen or eighteen feet long. We paid the rental fee and the guy was just about to push us away from the dock when I said, "is there anything special I should know?"

He stopped and looked at me and said, "have you never sailed before?"

"No"

He said, "oh shit," but it was too late he had already pushed me off.

It took me at least two hours to get the hang of it. After I finally understood the principle of the sails, I had fun with it. Owning a boat might be fun.

The next day, Dudley came by and said he had just talked to the bank manager and if we bought two boats, he would take off another five hundred a boat. I went to Marina Del Rey and rented a slip, and went to Downy and bought a boat. I wasn't surprised when Dudley never bought his boat. I was embarrassed about it, and never invited him to go sailing on my boat.

I enjoyed the boat for several years and kept it until I bought a larger boat with two cabins and all of the comforts of home. I had a head in the main cabin and a full galley. The back cabin also had a head. I knew what features I wanted and shopped until I found it. A center cockpit with two separate cabins was a great thing. Two couples could stay on the water for a week without getting in each-others way. I moved the boat to Ventura because there were four Islands instead of just Catalina off the coast there.

Like most toys, the romance of the boat faded away. I said to my wife that we had not had the boat out in a year and I was going to sell it. She said don't do that, let's use it. We went to Catalina for a week, and had a good time. When another year passed without us using the boat again, I sold it.

The auction in Little Rock was coming up and I had to start checking bloodlines of the mares in the sale. I had them mail me a catalog and I was checking out their pedigrees. The catalog had their breeding but they didn't seem to understand that the immediate family could affect the value of a mare by huge amounts. For example, a mare that was worth twenty-thousand who had a full sister or her dam foal a stakes winner might now be worth forty-thousand. A mare that had three colts without a winner that was worth ten thousand had a colt win a stake race a week before the auction might suddenly be worth fifty-thousand. You had to check a lot more than the little bit that was in the catalog.

I picked out eight mares that I would like to own but my bank account would have a lot to say about how many I actually bought. I would not buy horses on credit. That puts me in a position of having to sell and that is a slippery slope. If I think a horse is worth a certain amount, I want to be strong enough to try to get that amount. I don't want to have to sell him because I have a note coming due. The price at auctions had a lot to do with what buyers show up. I have been to auctions where every horse sold for ten percent more than he was worth. I have also been to auctions where the money men weren't there and every horse sold for twenty percent less than their worth. At those kinds of auctions, I spend my whole bank roll if I have to. It's money in the bank.

I took my six-horse trailer and drove to Little Rock. I went a day early so I could spend some time looking at the horses and I wanted a chance to talk to the lady. If there was no money at the sale, and the lady passed a lot of her horses out as not sold, it might be possible to work something out with her. You never know where you might talk yourself into a profit. I went to a private auction of thoroughbreds in Texas once, and the owner invited me into his home for lunch and proposed that I buy all of his horses and I didn't have to pay for them until I sold them. I didn't take him up on it because he had some horses, I didn't think I could sell. I just bought the horses I liked.

I spent all morning looking at her horses and talked to her about her ranch and her stallion. She had a lot of lookers, which didn't bode well for me. I looked at my watch and it was one o'clock and she was looking a little stressed out. I suggested that she take a little break and let me buy her lunch. She shouldn't kill herself today. Tomorrow is the important day. She started to say no and at the last minute changed her mind and said ok.

The last thing I wanted her to think was that I was hitting on her. This was strictly business and I was very careful about everything I said. I didn't want to say anything she could take wrong. She was an attractive lady with a braided pigtail two feet down her back but that wasn't why I was here.

We had lunch and I had a grilled cheese sandwich and she had a salad. I finally got her to talk about herself. Her name was Barbara and she had grown up on a ranch in Texas and had got interested in horses as a teen ager. Her father had a couple of race horses that won a few races at Sunland Park in El Paso. She had never had a desire to train race horses. She could see that it was a lot of work and a gypsy lifestyle that didn't really appeal to her. She had a quarter horse mare that she had done a little barrel racing with but didn't find that much fun either. She had bred her and had really enjoyed raising the baby and decided that was what she wanted to do. She had bought four mares from Kentucky and started studying blood lines. The problem was having to ship all the way to Kentucky to have the mares bred. She had done that for ten years before she found what she considered a stud prospect. Her broodmare band had grown to fifty mares and it was costing too much to breed all of them in Kentucky. She was going to make this big push to try to make her stud prospect into a known horse. He was a royal bred horse that had become entangled in a failed syndicate and had been tied up in the courts until he was six years old and too old to race. When she told me, who had put the syndicate together I believed the mess. I knew him well and everything he touched ended up in court. She was trying to prove her stud and at the same time reduce her broodmare band. Her father was complaining about the cost of her breeding farm. We went back to the barn and I told her that I would see her tomorrow.

The auction started at eleven and people were looking at the horses by seven in the morning. I brought her a coffee and I had a Dr Pepper since I don't like coffee. I asked her if she had breakfast and she said yes, she had a Macdonald's breakfast sandwich. She was trying to show every horse herself and she was going crazy. There were a few horses of other people's that I wanted to look at so I left her alone. I had looked at all of the horses that I was interested in before the auction started. I had marked all of the horses that I would take at a good price.

They started right on time. This was a mixed sale, which meant they had breeding stock and yearlings. There were four or five yearlings that I would buy if the price was right. I had bought a group of yearlings a couple of years ago here and made a nice profit on them. I would buy mares or yearlings at the right price. They would all make money if the price was right.

I had bought two yearlings before the first of the Texas mares came in to the ring. This was not one of the mares that I wanted but it would give me some idea of how her horses were going to sell. The first mare brought eight thousand and that was about two thousand over what I would have given. I was glad I didn't pass the two yearlings waiting for the mares. I might not get any of them bought. They sold four of her horses before one that I was interested in came in the ring. The auctioneer gave her too much of a buildup and I think he might have scared some of the bidders off. They might have thought that he was trying too hard to sell her and something might be wrong with her. I bought her for sixty-five hundred and marked her a steal. They sold two yearlings before the mare that I thought was the best of her offerings. I bought her for ten-thousand and marked her well bought. She would make a profit. She sold a mare that I didn't like near as well as my mare and she sold for sixteen-thousand. The prices were starting to climb and I might not be able to buy any more. Two of the mares that I wanted sold for more than I was willing to pay. There were only three more of the mares I had marked to buy. The first one of those that came into the ring sold for too much and then the money must have left because the bids stopped. I bought the other two that I wanted for sixty-five for one and seventy-two hundred for the other one. I had a trailer full and the only way I would buy more would be if I could buy at least four more. I couldn't come all the way back to pick them up unless I had at least four. I had money left and would see what the ones I had marked were bringing. The money must have run out because all of the horses were bringing a lot less. I bought two more mares for six-thousand apiece and three more yearlings.

I had to find a place to board the extra horses while I took my first load home. I had left horses at a ranch right outside of Little Rock a couple of years ago and I went to see if I could do it again. It had changed hands but the new people agreed to board my horses. I loaded those first and brought them out to the farm. I then went back and loaded the horses going home and got on the road. I was alone so I had to sleep enough to be safe driving. The rule I had for hauling horses was they had to be watered every three hours. If they weren't watered regularly, they had a tendency to get sick. The chore of watering the horses made the trip longer time wise, but it had to be done. It took me four days to get home and I was exhausted. I had a young man who galloped horses for me and I asked if he wanted to ride to Kentucky and back with me to pick up some horses and he said yes. The trip to Kentucky and back was better with another person along but it still took a week.

The yearlings would be turning two in three months, and I put them on grain and started breaking them to ride. It was great to have my own racetrack so I could do it right at home. The mares had been cleaned up for the sale so there was nothing to do with them and I put them out in paddocks. I called a few people to tell them that I had the mares and sat back to see if there was any interest.

It was about this time that I discovered Carlos Arruzo. A friend of mine called me and said hey, we have rented a box at the bull fights in Ensenada this weekend and I thought you might like to go because one of the guys is fighting from horse back. I had never been to a bull fight and had never heard of anyone fighting from horseback. It was a no brainer, of course I would like to go. The first surprise was the box. It was under the stands instead of on top of them. It was like a machinegun bunker with the opening across the front just a couple of feet above the fence around the arena. There were four of us and there was room for another four or five. We were right in the action. There is a lane that runs around the arena and matadors and other personnel are using that lane. There are entrances to the arena from that lane all around the arena. It was like we were a member of the crew.

I didn't know who Carlos Arruzo was so I didn't appreciate his fame. We had a couple of regular fights to start the show and having never seen a bull fight I found it interesting. Then Arruzo came in on horseback and he was riding an Andalusian horse trained like a dressage horse. He was trained to strut his stuff while moving forward or sideways. I was spellbound. It was a beautiful dance of death and Arruzo played it to perfection. He would taunt the bull into charging and move his horse at the last second. Just as it looked as if he had no chance of escaping the charge he would dance out of the way. After he had enthralled the entire stadium Arruzo dismounted and killed the bull. One of the guys said that in Spain and Mexico the rule was, once a bull had been fought in the ring he must be killed. There could be no chance that a bull who had been in the ring could by mistake come back to fight again. In Portugal, where this type of horseback fighting originated, the bull wasn't killed.

He fought one more time later in the day. He was mounted on a different Andalusian horse that was trained just as well as the first one. I would not have missed an Arruzo fight for the rest of my life but I only got to see him two more times before he was killed in a car wreck. His performance was as beautiful as the ballet.

He was a very interesting man. After I had seen him fight, I started researching him. At one time he and a great Spanish fighter named Manolete were competing to be called the greatest bullfighter in the world. It was a competition that carried over many seasons. Arruzo was for sure the greatest Mexican Matador of all time, but he wanted the title of best in the world. They kept making there fights more spectacular and thus more dangerous until Manolete was finally gored and died from his wounds. That left Arruzo the un-challenged best in the world.

He was so famous that it is hard to separate facts from myths. The story goes that he was hired to do the fighting in a movie. The director, who knew little about bull fighting, wanted Arruzo to perform things that were unsafe. He was gored and several Matadors were gored trying to protect Arruzo. It left him with one arm shorter than the other and he retired. With time on his hands he ended up learning to fight horse-back in Portugal. This launched him on a new career and put him back in the spotlight.

I had a call from the owner of a farm in Napa Valley that was interested in one of my mares. I had posted the mares on the internet and waited to see if any one liked their breeding. This gentleman was interested in the one that I thought was the best and I had given the most money for. He asked the price and I told him I would take twenty-five-thousand for her. I explained that if she wasn't in foal to an unknown horse, I would have asked thirty-five-thousand. He said that he was in Woodland Hills and could be here in about half hour if that was ok. I told him I was just hanging out and to come on over. I was sitting in the office in the barn browsing the extended pedigrees of my mares and listening to music tapes. He drove up and I didn't want to seem too eager and the office was clearly marked so I just sat and let him come to me.

I had a Gary Moore album playing down and dirty blues when he walked in. He listened for a couple of minutes and said, "I see you listen to the devil's music."

"I do. Do you know how it became known as the devil's music?"

"I never thought about it. Do you mean there was a particular reason it was called the devil's music?"

"There was, and it was wrapped up with religion and money. Blues was played in black bars called joints from Memphis down through Mississippi and all over the south. Every little town had at least one of those joints usually just outside of the town so they didn't bother any of the citizens and weren't bothered by the cops. The music was primarily black blues from the cotton fields. The folks came to listen and dance and forget their hard life. These joints were usually not bothered by the police and didn't have many rules. It was common for the music to play as long as there were people dancing and drinking and that could, on Saturday night, go to three or four in the morning. The men would come home about daylight and collapse in bed. There was no way they were going to get up and go to church. The preachers faced with dwindling collection plates started labeling it as the devil's music because it was keeping the men out of the church. They thought if they labeled it that way it would scare the women into stopping their husband from going to the joints. It didn't work that way, but it was known for ever more as the devil's music."

I handed him a sheet showing her pedigree back three generations and a sheet showing the same for the horse she was bred to. I had left her in the paddock because I wanted him to see the other mares. I took a halter and a lead shank and said she is over here. And he followed me over to the paddock. I pointed her out and let him walk in the paddock for a closer look. I noticed that he was looking at the other mares as he walked through them. He stopped about ten feet from her and looked her over. I will put a halter on her if you want to look her over close up. He said would you please do that, and I walked over and slipped the halter on. He didn't know that I had caught her about twenty times and always gave her a sugar cube. He walked around looking at her from every angle.

I was glad she was gentle because he picked up her feet and looked at them. I didn't Know how much he knew about what he was looking at, but she was a great looking mare. She had great confirmation and a pretty head. I didn't say a word during the inspection. I only answer questions during this part of the sale. I have seen people talk themselves out of a sale instead of into it. I had six mares in this paddock and four yearlings in the paddock next to it. I had sold one of the mares already. One of the mares that I gave sixty-five-hundred for I had sold for eight-thousand.

He asked me who the other mares were in foal to and when I told him that all but one were in foal to the same horse, I had to tell him the story of the lady buying well-bred mares trying to prove her stud. I told him I would have bought more of them but my bank-roll is not unlimited.

He asked if he could take a look at the breeding on the other mares. Since I had hoped that he might be interested in one of the others I had folded them and had them in my back pocket. I gave them to him, and as he looked at the pedigrees, he asked which mare fit each pedigree. He asked the price on a mare I had given eight-thousand for and I priced her at twelve thousand. The next one he asked for a price was one I had given sixty-five hundred for and I priced her at nine-thousand. He looked at the three mares one more time and turned to me and said, "I will give forty-thousand for those three mares."

I thought about it for a couple of minutes and said, "that's hitting me pretty hard but I would do the deal for forty-two."

He put out his hand and said, "I can meet that price. Let's go to the office and I will give you a check but it might be two or three days before my guy can get down to pick them up."

He wrote me a check and I asked him, "do you want the papers now?"

He said, "no, send them with the horses. They need to be on file at the farm and I have a habit of misplacing things."

He shook my hand again and drove away. It wasn't three o'clock yet and I went to the bank to deposit the check, the horses weren't sold until that check cleared.

It was three days before the guy called me from the farm to ask for directions. After I gave him directions and hung up, I pulled my account up on my phone and the check was no longer listed as pending. It had been deposited to my account. I wasn't worried about it, but it was still nice to see it had turned into cash.

The van driver found me with no trouble and we got them loaded without mishap. I gave the driver a manila envelope with the papers and the pedigree sheets in it. He was on his way and I had several free horses. The load was paid for with a profit and everything left was more profit. I always like it when that happens.

I was curious how Barbara had fared at the auction so I gave her a call. We talked a few minutes before I asked about money. I didn't beat around the bush. I started with the big question. "How much did the program of getting your stud's foals out there cost you?"

I wasn't sure she would tell me, but she did. "I just ran my numbers yesterday and adding what I lost on the mares and all of my expenses it came to a few dollars under three-hundred-thousand-dollars. My father is going to have a heart attack when he sees these numbers."

"Do you honestly think it was worth the money?"

"It depends on what angel you approach it from. I am going to breed my mares to this horse and if I get a runner or two out there it will increase the value of his foals tremendously. Plus, I have spent twice that amount for the last couple of years in stud fees in Kentucky. My defense with my father is that he told me to reduce my brood mare band."

She said, "it must be karma, I was looking for your phone number this morning because I wanted to ask you about this blood-stock agent that called me from California. He thinks he can put a syndicate together on my Stud. I am not sure what he is trying to do here, but he has called twice to tell me about the big deals he has brokered."

"I have one piece of advice about him. Don't walk away from him, RUN! He is a Lawyer's dream. The only people making any money from his deals are the attorneys. This is the same guy who kept your stud from racing by having him tied up in court. I was at a Kentucky horse sale and a marshal found out I was from California and came over to ask about him. During the conversation he told me he had over thirty subpoenas to serve on him if he ever caught him in Kentucky. I was in the office at Santa Anita picking up my papers at the end of the meet when one of the clerks asked the racing secretary what he should do with the papers on one of his syndicated horses that had just won a major stake race. The secretary told him to leave them until the court decided who should get them."

She said, "I'm glad I asked you about him."

I added, "I had bought a nice Swaps mare at a bargain price of ten-thousand and he calls me up. He tells me that he has a buyer for her for thirty-thousand and he wants a commission of ten percent. The catch was that my place wasn't fancy enough to show her and he wanted to move her. I said not without paying for her first. I never heard from him again. Later a friend of mine asked if I had sold the mare yet? I told him I had sold her and he asked if I got the eighty-thousand the agent was asking for her. He is really bad news."

We talked a few more minutes and ended on a friendly note. She was someone I would put on my Christmas card list.

I had driven to Griffith Park to look at a horse which

turned out to not be worth the price the lady wanted for him. I stopped by the stable of a friend of mine when I saw his car parked out front. There were five of them playing gin in the office. They were all in the business and sort of mutual friends. These get to gathers weren't really about playing cards. They were mostly about swapping gossip and maybe about buying or selling a horse. I sat down to watch and listen to the gossip.

One of the guys asked me if I knew a guy named Phillip Roth?

I said, "I do, what do you want to know about him?"

He said, "he stopped by my place yesterday and I have never met him before. Where do you know him from?"

"I first met him two or three years ago at a sale in Caldwell Idaho. Then I met him again a couple of years ago at a sale in Hermiston Oregon. Since then I have run into him several times in different places. I have even seen him at the sale here a couple of times. He has a place up near San Francisco. He seems to be a straight shooter and he has a deal we all would like to have. He has a blank check with a bank to buy anything he wants to buy. He strikes me as a man of ambition who doesn't recognize the word, enough."

One of the other guys piped in, "I would like to have a deal like that. I wonder how he got that done?"

I looked at him like he was stupid and said, "all you

need is a piece of property worth half a million that is paid for, and the bank will give you the same deal."

The guys around the table all laughed and he went back to looking at his cards. They were talking about cars when I first came in and one of the guys looked at me and asked, "if I remembered my first car?"

I said, "yes I do, it was a forty-eight Mercury and it smoked like a steam engine. The compression was so bad that I parked it in a grocery store parking lot and left it in reverse. When I came back it had creeped all the way across the parking lot."

"What did you do with it?"

"I was in St Louis going to Washington University and had discovered I couldn't afford it. A couple of friends were in California and had told me about their junior Colleges that were free. I decided that the first two years for free was a deal I couldn't pass up. I called a cab company and asked what the cab fare was from where I lived to the Greyhound bus station down town. They told me it would be twenty-five dollars. I went by a local wrecking yard and he offered me thirty dollars for my car. The numbers didn't compute, so I drove my car to the bus station and parked in the parking lot. I left the keys in the ignition and left the signed title laying on the dashboard. I got on the bus and never looked back."

"Did you leave them a full tank of gas?"

"As a matter of fact, I was scared to death I was going

to run out of gas before I got there."

That got a laugh from everyone.

"What are all of you guys doing here. Don't any of you work anymore? Any of you have something that might interest me for sale? Any of you need something for a customer that I might have? I waited for a couple of minutes for someone to speak up, before I said, "I can't hang around here with a bunch of dead beats. I need to go where people are trying to do something. I'll see you guys later." I walked out and drove away.

I tried to touch base with all of the guys who had a stable of some kind at least once every month or two. On the way home I would drive close to a guy who had a little operation that I hadn't seen in three or four months. I had sold him four or five horses spread over the last year or two. I decided it was time I checked up on him. As I turned into the drive at his place a man and his wife were walking out to their car and Josh was standing by the door of his little office watching them leave. When he saw me, he yelled at them to stop and they turned around with a bewildered look. He motioned them to come back and as they walked back; he came out to meet them. I closed the door on my pickup and stood waiting to see what was going on. They met him about ten yards from where I was standing and I heard him say, this is the guy I was telling you about.

The three of them walked over to me and he said,

"Graham, these people are interested in buying a thoroughbred mare. I told them that you were the only one around here that might have one for sale."

I put out my hand and said, "Hi, I'm Graham Peterson. What are you looking for?"

They both shook my hand while he was saying, "I'm Ralph Sikes and this is my wife Betty. We have a place in Rolling Hills and thought we might enjoy raising a foal or two."

Rolling Hills was built as a horse community and had small horse barns behind every home and bridle-trails throughout the community. It was really nice and very expensive. "Are you familiar with Thoroughbred breeding?"

His wife spoke up and said, "he better be. He has sat up until midnight every night for the last six months going over breeding records and books and manuals."

I said. "that's what it takes to know what you are doing. Otherwise you will end up with a bunch of five-hundred-dollar mares that you paid ten-thousand each for. That's not a good thing."

He said, "do you have a couple of mares we could look at?"

"I do, and I am on my way home right now if you would like to follow me."

He shook his head yes and I got into my truck and waited for them to get in their car. When we drove in at the ranch the exercise boy was galloping one of the yearlings on the race track. Actually, as of the first of the year they are now considered to be two years old. The driveway went around the end of the racetrack back to the barn We both parked in front of the barn and I invited them into the office to look at the breeding of the four mares that I had on hand.

I gave him a sheet on each mare with a three-generation family tree on it and said, "I'll give you a few minutes to see if there is anything you are interested in breeding wise and we will go look at the mares."

He sat down in a chair and really looked through the breeding. Since two of the mares were in foal to the horse in Texas, I had included his pedigree also. He spent about a half-hour reading the pedigrees and said, "I hope these mares are not too expensive for me."

"I don't think they will be. I try to price my horses to sell them. It is very rare to find one of my horses overpriced."

We walked out to the paddock where the four mares were. They were all four showing that they were for sure in foal. Since they were all young mares, they didn't have their bellies stretched to the point of looking droopy. Being in foal just made them look fat and happy.

He handed me two sheets and asked which ones were these two. They were both from Texas and I pointed them out. He walked around the two mares for about ten minutes before he chose one to ask me the price of.

I said, "I can sell you either one of those mares at a discount of their true value because they are carrying a Stallion's first crop. I will take nine thousand for either one of them, and I promise you if they were in foal to a proven stud, they would be fifteen-thousand plus whatever the stud-fee had been."

I like the one he didn't pick best, but I wasn't going to tell him that. He walked around the mares again and he and his wife walked away to have a private conversation. He came back after the conversation and said, "would you take fifteen-thousand for both of them?"

"They are too well-bred for that, but if it will help you any, I'll take off a thousand. That's five-hundred per mare. That's the best I can do. I would wear the tires off my truck trying to replace them for that price."

He looked at his wife and she must have given a secret nod because he turned back and said, "if you will deliver them, we have a deal."

"I can deliver them today if you would like, or I can give you a day or two if you need to get your barn ready for them."

"Just give me an hour to bed the stalls and bring them on."

We went to the office and he gave me a check and I gave him the registration papers on the two mares. I took the address from his check and put it into my GPS. It was going to be twice as time consuming if I got caught in the after-work crowd on the streets. I didn't wait an hour. I caught the mares, brushed them off a little and put them in the trailer and got on the road. I was only a half hour behind him, but that was enough time to bed two stalls. My GPS took me right to him without a hitch and I was back home in three hours.

The yearlings I had bought in Little Rock had been galloping for three months and were going really well. I would go to Fairplex tomorrow and make arrangements for stalls for them. They were now two-year olds and I needed them at the track in order to sell them. I liked to bring my babies up to the point of working and sell them at that time. Galloping didn't cause leg problems and they normally didn't get any soreness until you started putting speed on them. They were broke to ride and handle on the track and they were trained to not fight the walking machine. The only thing they weren't trained for yet was the starting gate. That is the only thing I don't have but I would start that part of their training as soon as I got them to the track. Another month or two and I would start looking for customers for them.

Billy, my exercise rider usually started about nine in the morning and I waited to talk to him before I left in the morning. I asked him if he would be able to go and live at the race track for two or three months. I told him he could live in the tack room so he wouldn't have any rent and I would pay him three hundred a week. He jumped right on that. He probably would have done it for free just to be at the racetrack. I went by the bank and deposited the check from the sale of the mares and went on to Pomona and got four stalls. My trainer's licenses had expired but I didn't need to renew it unless I decided to race one of these colts myself.

On the way I stopped to see a good friend of mine that had a western wear store. He sold tack and whatever caught his eye but mostly boots and cloths. He had a huge store In Woodland Hills.

I had first met him when he decided to become a horse trader. He had rented a place near me and bought six or eight horses to resale. He had discovered that you can't sell horses if you aren't there to sell them. He had a store to run and couldn't go and show people the horses. He had first tried to hire me to sell them for him and I of course declined. He then hired some old guy that I guess came into his store and told him he was a horseman. That didn't work out very well for several reasons, one being he didn't know anything about horses and another being he was never sober after ten o'clock in the morning.

John finally called me one day and told me to stop and look at the horses and make him an offer for the whole bunch. I discovered that he was almost impossible to deal with. I realized after I got to know him that he had a hang up about selling anything. I made him an offer which he immediately turned down. He asked me twice what I had just offered him and I told him he was nuts and started to leave.

He stopped me at the door and said, "have you tried the new diner they just put in up the street?"

They had brought in a railroad dining car and made a restaurant out of it. I told him, "I hadn't tried it yet."

He said, "let's go give it a try." I should mention that he was a good doer and weighed about three- hundred and fifty pounds.

I said, "why not?" and we went to the car.

It had just started to rain and he turned on his wind-shield wipers. We parked in front of the diner and walked in. There were only a few people in the diner and one of them was Dr. Fischbeck. He was an older gentleman who did the weather on one of the big channels there in Los Angeles. He tried to give his show a little pizazz by acting a little of the wall but he insisted that every one called him Doctor. He was sitting by himself and as we walked by his table John says to me, "did you notice that it is raining even though the weather man said sunny all day."

Fischbeck leaped up grabbed his chair and flung it down the aisle as far as he could throw it. He yelled at the top of his voice, "I am god damn tired of these people always complaining about my weather forecast."

I walked on back to a table and hoped that the good Doctor had noticed that John made three of him. I guess he did because he stormed out of the restaurant without saying another word. I don't think he had ordered yet, there was nothing on his table.

John came back and sat down, "do you think he might be a little thinned skin?"

A waitress came back and picked up the chair and put it back at the table before she came to our table. I said to her, "He is a terrible tipper, you didn't lose anything."

I ordered a hamburger and fries and John ordered everything on the menu. When she walked away and he had me as a captive audience he said, "I can't take that for those horses. I need to sell them but I can't sell them that cheap."

I said, "John, I need to give you some facts about horse trading. The profit or loss in a horse deal is set when you buy the horse. If you buy him too high there is no profit. The guys that operate on the greater fool theory don't make it in the horse business."

He interrupted me to ask, "what is the greater fool theory?"

"For you to think that it doesn't matter what you pay for the horse, someone will be fool enough to pay more. It doesn't work that way. The critical factor is they eat. Let me give you a good example of the trap you step into by not factoring that in.

I was coming back from a Kentucky horse auction. Going through Glendale, Arizona I saw a very nice-looking place with a Horse for Sale sign out in front. I pulled in and an older gentleman showed me two horses. They were decent horses and I could have sold them for maybe three hundred each. The problem was he asked four hundred apiece. I had to pass. A year later coming back from the sale in Kentucky he still had the sign out and I stopped again. He showed me the same two horses and asked me the same four hundred dollars apiece. I keep really good books on my operation and it cost me twenty-five dollars a month to keep a horse. Think about the fact that he now had at least another three hundred dollars in each of those horses. If he had to have four hundred in the beginning, he now had to have seven hundred. Since he couldn't sell them for four hundred, he sure wasn't going to get seven.

Let's say he bought the horses for two hundred apiece he now had five hundred in each of them. He was going to lose money no matter what he did at this point and he was going to lose twenty-five more every month he kept each horse. If he still had them next year when I came by, he would have eight hundred each in them. My point is, he was losing money he could never recover. I see guys doing this every day and they don't last long in the horse business. They insist on a profit on every horse they buy. They hold a horse for three months to make a twenty-five-dollar profit and don't realize they lost fifty-dollars on the deal. As soon as I decide I have paid too much for a horse I get rid of him. I have made a bad investment and lost my money. I don't like losing more money by holding on to him.

I'm not saying you need to sell those horses to me, but I am saying you need to sell them to someone. To tell you the truth, I was doing you a favor when I made you the offer. Because you are a friend, I offered just what I thought I could get for them. I really don't want the horses. I was just trying to help you out."

Our food came and we both got busy eating. I could see the wheels turning while his jaws worked. He was calculating what he had in the horses and what they were costing him. How large his loss was and how fast it was growing. I didn't say a word. I had given him all of the advice I could and it was up to him to make his decision.

I actually had offered him a little more than they were worth because I had another out. I had a couple of clients that operated summer camps and always rented horses from me for the summer. It wasn't a gold mine but it was ninety dollars a horse for the summer. A dollar a day made the horses cheaper and I sold them at the end of the summer.

We had finished eating and he still hadn't said any-thing about the horses. He went to the restroom and when he came back, he said, "here is the deal I just had a load of hay delivered a few days ago and I think I have enough for about a month. I am going to make a big push to sell the horses at a retail price. I will run ads in the newspaper and really make an effort. If I haven't sold them by the time my feed runs out, I will sell them to you."

"You had to go sit in the restroom to figure that out?"

"I like to think in privacy."

"I've got to go. You've wasted too much of my time. Are you getting the check?"

"I don't want to, but I guess I owe you that much for the business lesson."

I walked out before I remembered we had come in his car. I started to go back in and I saw him ordering desert. I thought what the hell, it is only three blocks and it had quit raining. I walked back to my car. I was glad about him keeping them on his feed for a month. That was one of the negatives about the deal. I was going to have to feed them for two months. It would now be cut to just a month.

I went back to the barn and we loaded the tack and a folding cot into the back of the truck. We loaded the four colts in the trailer and took them to Fairplex. We had the horses unloaded and put away before dark. We had the kid in the tack room all squared away and I told him I would see him in the morning.

I set my alarm really early. I had to drive all the way

to Pomona and I wanted to be there by seven o'clock. I made it by seven-thirty which wasn't bad. I showed Billy around. I took him up to the kitchen and showed him where the restroom and showers were. I walked him over to the chute coming onto the track. They had a two-horse starting gate with no doors on it about half way down the chute. I told him I wanted him to walk the colts in and stand for a minute or two every morning on the way to the track. I had a walker at the ranch so they didn't have to learn how to walk on the machine.

I told him that I wanted to gallop each colt two miles every morning. I didn't want any speed put on at any time. There is always someone looking for a horse to work with. If you ever let them talk you into doing it, I will fire you on the spot. I will not be here every morning, but when I am here, I will be in the grandstand watching the horses gallop. I expect you to handle my horses in a professional manner, and if I see you not doing that, I will fire you immediately. I didn't go back until Friday morning and true to my word I sat in the corner of the grandstand until he was finished. I walked over to the barn and looked at the horses and took him to the kitchen for lunch. He seemed alright and was handling the horses ok. I talked with him for a while and payed him for the week.

I have a twenty-six-foot travel trailer and Fairplex has a RV park right next to the barn area. I had already tired of that long drive and decided I would bring my trailer out and spend a night or two here every week. I went over and talked to the stall man and he gave me a spot for my trailer.

I didn't have time to bring my trailer out and set it up until Tuesday. It was nice having it there. I knew a lot of the guys stabled there and it didn't take long to renew old friendships. I was letting them know that I wasn't here to go racing. I was just getting them ready to sell. With them knowing they were for sale they would watch them train and might like one or two of them.

At the end of the month John called me to pick up his horses. He had not sold a single horse. He was down on horse trading and had realized it was more complicated than he thought.

He was off on another money-making scheme. Right after the big gas shortage, and the long lines at the gas pumps, for some reason California experienced uncommon inflation. The most radical inflation occurred in real estate. Real estate was going up daily. He being the classic opportunist, jumped right on that.

He was prowling neighborhoods and making offers on houses. When he got a hit, he would put two-hundred down to open escrow. He would then put the house up for sale and sell it with a double escrow. According to him, he was making from five-hundred to three or four-thousand per house. He claimed that he was averaging ten-thousand a month profit. I asked what did he do when he couldn't sell the house. He said he only had two hundred invested so he just walked away, and it had only happened once.

I thought it over and decided that I already had too many balls in the air. I had in the last few years bought and sold half a dozen houses but I didn't buy them to speculate on the market rise. I actually like working on them and do a remodel before I put them up for sale. I tell my friends that I don't hunt or fish and working on an old house is my relaxation. Since I only work on them in my spare time it usually takes several months to do the remodel. I have made money on every house I've sold.

I have already faced the results of too many irons in the fire. At one time I had a boarding-stables, and at the same time I had a Mobile gas station and at the same time I had a catering truck with a full route. Suddenly there came a morning that I couldn't get out of bed. I was working from four o'clock in the morning until ten o'clock at night and one morning when the alarm went off at three-thirty I couldn't get out of bed. I could hear the alarm but I couldn't get up. It was as if my body wouldn't move and it scared me. I thought I was having a stroke or a heart attack or something. It was noon before things started working and I could get out of bed. I wasted no time divesting myself of the catering truck and it took a little longer to sell the gas station. I now make short term investments, but I make sure that they don't require full time supervision. Having three business that all needed full time supervision nearly killed me.

It was about this time that I made my wife so mad she didn't speak to me for a month. It was over a simple thing I sold her corvette. There was more to it of course than me deciding one day to sell her car. It started out in a normal way. She had decided that her Corvette needed a paint job. She shopped around and chose a shop that was going to paint her car for six-hundred-dollars. To put that in perspective, Earl Scheib was painting cars for forty-nine dollars at that time. I agreed to the paint job and she had it painted. They told her not to wash it for a week and she had the hose in her hand on the eighth day. A couple of days later she told me that she had found a run in the paint and the company was going to repaint the car for her. On the eighth day she was out in the drive with her hose. A couple of days later she said they had missed a spot under the bottom of the windshield wiper and they were going to repaint it again. The third time must have done the deed because she didn't say any more about it.

Three or four months later I ran into a deal where a strange man buying a horse from me that was not a registered horse insisted that I show him proof that I had purchased and owned the horse. I had not received a receipt for the horse but I had written on the check what the check was for. I was looking through a box of canceled checks and I came across three canceled checks for six-hundred-dollars each for paint jobs on a sixty-eight Corvette. I didn't even tell her

I had found the checks. I just took the car down and sold it. I said she didn't speak to me for a month but it might have been longer.

She had her revenge though. She bought an Austin Healy that cost more than I sold the Corvette for.

I went over and picked up the horses I am buying from John early the next morning. I was unloading the last of them when Dudley drove up and parked in front of the barn. He walked up and said, "hey what's going on? Did you miss me?"

"How can I miss you when you won't go away?"

That made no impression on him and he said, "I'm planning a trip to Hong Kong, and thought you might be ready for another trip."

"If that is an invitation, my reply is, not in my life time."

He shook his head in a negative way and said, "I can't believe how long you hold a grudge."

"I don't have a grudge against you. I have just taken your name off of my Christmas Card list, that's all."

He stood there for a minute trying to think of how to go from here. He finally said, "I just thought I should ask. It's going to be a fun trip. By the way, the live band at the Captain's Table at the marina, is really good. If you are down that way you should stop by. I'll see you later." He got into his car and drove away.

I had decided that I would drive down to the track tonight and be there in the morning. I was expecting the later part of the week to be fairly busy and I might not have a chance to get there. I got there just about dark and I had stopped to buy a few groceries. I was making a grilled cheese sandwich when someone knocked on the door.

I didn't recognize the guy standing at the door and asked, "how can I help you?"

He said, "my name is Harley Hebert and I heard you have some babies for sale. I saw your light on and I have tried to catch you at the barn but I've had no luck."

I asked, "do you want to talk about them tonight, or come to the barn in the morning. I will be there for sure and you can look them over."

"I am interested in the horses but there is no need to waste your time showing them to me if I can't afford them."

"Are you interested in one or all of them?"

"I am interested in all of them if they are in my price range."

I figured that I had eighteen hundred dollars apiece in them by now including all of my expenses." I will take three-thousand each. Take one or take all." That is really cheap for a race horse and I hope it doesn't scare him off.

He said, "I will be at the barn at eight in the morning

to look them over. We might do some business."

I set my alarm for six because I wanted to get to the barn before the kid went to the track with them. I went to the kitchen for a fried egg sandwich at seven and the kid was there having breakfast. I explained that we weren't going to the track today because someone wanted to look at the horses.

Harley arrived at eight sharp and went over the horses very completely. He felt every joint and watched each horse walk and trot.

When he was finished, he came over and said, "here is my offer. I will give the three-thousand each for these two colts and I will give twenty-five each for the other two."

I knew that I could hold on until they had a little more training and get more money. I would have more money in them and could at any time lose one to an accident. "I am going to sell them to you and I wish you good luck."

I was really surprised when he went to his truck and came back with eleven-thousand dollars in cash. It was just luck that I had their papers in my briefcase. I didn't normally carry registration papers any more since I had my car broken into several years ago, and a briefcase stolen with about twenty sets of papers in it. It took me months to get replacements from the Jockey Club. I had to send photos and fill out all kinds of paperwork on each horse. Two of them I had to blood type. It was a mess. The real damage was that I had to care for and feed them for three or four months longer than I intended.

As soon as I produced the papers, he made a call to someone to bring the trailer over to pick up the horses. They were at the barn in a half-hour and we loaded the horses with no mishaps. He said he was going to Thistle Downs with them. They should fit in there really well.

I could see that Billy was really disappointed about his racetrack experience being over so soon. I told him not to worry we would do it again real soon but he didn't look as though he believed me. He was most disappointed about having to move back home so I asked him if he would like to live in the trailer if I brought it over to the ranch and he jumped on that idea.

We loaded all of the tack and equipment in the truck and I hooked up to the trailer and we made the move in one load. When we reached the farm, I called a friend of mine to come and put in a septic tank for the trailer. Since he was doing it on the quite with no per-mit, he was able to do it in one day and Billy was all set.

It seems just when you get everything worked out and your life is going smooth, a new crisis jumps up. It was Saturday and an average day. I paid the Mexicans and took them to the store for their weekly shopping. They had a ritual that everyone I ever had working for me followed. They would cash their check and buy their food for the week and buy a money order with what was left and send it home to Mexico. Anyone that thinks they pump their pay checks into our economy, has never worked with them.

I was watching TV and about half asleep when there came a banging on the door. I got up and opened it to find one of my workers in a state of agitation. Fortunately, it was the one who spoke pretty good English or I would never have understood him. The gist of the matter was that the other worker was hurt really bad and needed a doctor. I assumed that a horse had kicked him or something. I went up to the barn with him and found the worker beat to a pulp and unconscious. I called for an ambulance and went up to the entrance to wait so I could show them where he was.

The guys with the ambulance were not very forthcoming about his condition and may have thought I did it. They took him away with the lights and siren on and wouldn't even tell me where they were taking him.

This was the first time I had a chance to talk to Jose and I asked him if he did this, and he said no. I asked him to show me his hands and he did. There was not a mark on them so I was sure he didn't do it. Whoever did this was going to have messed up knuckles.

It was a long drawn out conversation before I had all of the facts. It turns out that there is a little Mexican Mafia that goes around collecting part of the pay checks from all of the illegals for not turning them in to immigration. My guys had been giving them twenty each for a couple of months. The one who was beat up went by the name of Tete. I don't know what that means but it was his name. He had refused to pay them this week and they beat him up.

Jose didn't know anything about the gang. He didn't know any of their names and he didn't know where they came from. He didn't know how they had found him and Tete since they don't associate with anyone else. He said they just showed up one payday a couple of months ago and demanded twenty dollars a week for not turning them into immigration. He did say that the guy who drove the truck they came in was a white guy. He never got out of the truck but he was definitely white. I told him if they came back to get the license number of the truck.

I hung around the stable all morning because I knew at some point the police were going to come for a visit. They showed up about ten and I was surprised that it was two uniformed officers in a black and white. I had expected a couple of detectives.

I soon realized why they had sent patrol officers. I could tell right away that they assumed it was an open and shut case. I had beat up one of my workers for whatever reason and they had just come out to arrest me. They didn't ask any questions and put me in the back of the car and took me to the Van Nuys police station. At least they didn't handcuff me.

We arrived at the station and the officers led me to the counter and said to the duty officer, "that I was to be booked for assault."

I said, "hold on a minute. I haven't done anything but call an ambulance. I wasn't even there when this guy got beat up. I want to see a detective and get this straightened out. There is not going to be any booking of me. Especially by two cops that didn't ask anyone any questions."

The duty officer looked at the officer that had said book him and raised his eyebrows as if to say what do you want to do. "Detective Capa is the one who sent me out to talk to this guy."

"Talk, is the key word here. The only thing this guy said to me, was get in the car. Now he wants to book me for something. I want to see Detective Capa."

The duty officer picked up the phone and dialed someone. He talked for a couple of minutes before he hung up the phone and said, "Capa wants to see him. Take him on up."

They took me up to the second floor and to a desk with a short, wide detective. He was dressed in gray slacks and a blue stripped shirt with a tie loosened and his top button undone. He said to me, "have a seat." Then he said, "thanks guys I got this from here."

He looked me over for a couple of minutes before he said, "the duty officer said you seemed upset about the cops who brought you in. You want to tell me about it?"

"Look, two crimes have been committed against this poor guy and I have nothing to do with either one. I told the duty officer that these two cops came to my place and said get in the car. No problem, I get in the car. We walk in the door downstairs and he tells the guy at the counter to book me for assault. Do you think I should not be upset? I haven't assaulted anyone and he didn't bother to ask me or to figure that out. I overheard him tell his partner that he would call immigration to pick up my other worker. How stupid is that? He is the only witness and the only person that can identify these guys."

He sat looking at me as if he couldn't decide whether to interview me or throw me in the drunk tank. He finally said, "why don't you tell me what is going on here. The only information I have is that the hospital called me this morning to report a man had been beaten so badly he was in a coma and very likely would not survive."

I said, "here is what I know at this point. About midnight last night there was someone pounding on my door. It was one of my two workers and he told me the other worker was hurt really bad. They live in an apartment attached to the barn. I went back to the barn and found the one worker badly beaten and unconscious. I called for an ambulance and went up to the street to wait for them so I could show them where he was. They came and picked him up and treated me like a criminal. They wouldn't even tell me where they were taking him. After they left, I questioned my other worker and found out that three men, one of them Mexican had been demanding twenty dollars a week from each of them for not calling immigration. It had been going on for several months and Tete refused to pay them this week. He didn't know the three guys and didn't know where they came from. The only thing he could tell me was that they came in a white truck and a white man was driving. The driver never got out of the truck."

 About half way through my story he started writing down some things down. He asked, "do you know if any other horsemen are having this problem?"

"Until last night I didn't know I had the problem. How could I know other people had the problem? You can bet your ass I will start asking around now though.

"Are you sure your boys didn't get in an argument?"

"The first thing I did was ask him to show me his hands and there wasn't a mark on them. You don't beat someone like that and not skin up all of your knuckles."

He said, "your right and I hadn't thought about that. How about showing me your knuckles."

I spread my hands out in front of him and he said, "I was only joking but I am glad to see they are clean. I think that's all I need from you for now. Here is my card, if you hear anything else give me a call."

"Since your guys brought me here do you think one of them might take me back to Chatsworth."

"That sounds fair." He picked up the phone and called the duty officer and told him to have someone take me home.

When I got home, I drove over to a good friend of mine who had been in the business for a long time. He used all Mexican help and I had too much work for one person. I wanted to know if he knew of anyone that had an extra hand right now that he didn't need. He told me he had three and only needed one and I could have two if I needed them. I didn't need but one right now and Art told one of the guys to pack up his stuff and go with me.

While we were waiting for him to get his things together Art asked me to look at a young foal that was not doing well. He had a nice paddock with a mare and foal in it and the foal was skin and bones. He said, "I have tried everything I can think of and nothing helps. Every morning when I come out, I expect to see him dead."

We were looking over the fence and I said, "I am really disappointed in you. As long as you have had horses and you would make a mistake like this."

Across the entire back of the paddock was a row of Oleander bushes about head high. He still didn't get the significance of that and I said, "you are poisoning the poor little bastard with that Oleander."

"I'll be damned, I had forgot that Oleander was poison." Just as he said that the foal walked over to the bush and started chewing on one of the leaves. I helped him move the mare and foal into the barn and he called me a couple of weeks later to tell me the colt was doing fine and gaining weight.

I took the guy back to the barn and turned him over to Jose. He didn't speak much English and it would take a while for him to learn the ropes. I gave him a couple of days before I asked Jose if he was going to be all right. Jose said he was a good worker so we were good.

As I was driving around, I asked everywhere I stopped if they would question their Mexican workers about someone holding them up for part of their pay. I figured that the guys would be like me and not realize it was happening.

I was out of thoroughbred horses and was out in the Chino area and decided to stop at Rex Ellsworth's ranch. I had bought a horse or two from his ranch manager. Rex was at the top of his game during that time. He had Swaps and Candy Spots and a whole barn full of good horses. His culls were better than most people's first string. Last year I had bought a four-year-old colt that hadn't broke his maiden here in California. I gave a thousand for him and sold him for two-thousand to a guy going to Phoenix. He broke his maiden first out for three-thousand claiming. The bottom claiming here was ten-thousand.

The farm manager had a nice little house on the edge of the ranch. There was a pickup in the driveway and I pulled in behind it. There were two big dogs laying in the front yard. I had no idea if the dogs were dangerous or not, so I eased the door open keeping my eyes on them. They both just lay there watching me and made no move to come and check me out. I walked slowly by the dogs and they just watched me walk by. I stepped up on the porch and they just watched me. I knocked on the door and there was no answer. I waited a couple of minutes and knocked again and there was still no answer. I had to admit no one was at home. I turned to leave and the dogs met me at the steps showing a lot of teeth and growling. I backed up and they both sat down and went silent. I talked to them for a few minutes and tried to come off the porch again. They turned into all teeth and ass holes as soon as I approached the step. I backed up again and they sat down as if I had given the command to sit.

I sat on the porch leaning against the wall for two hours before his wife drove up in her car. She apologized for their behaver and told me they had done the same thing to the Fedex man a week ago. She said he was really mad and told her there would never be another delivery from Fedex. They had a do not deliver list and her address was going to be on it.

On the way home I tried to call back on calls I had received while I was captured on the porch. My phone was in the car and I could hear it ring but I couldn't do anything about it. The first two calls were both from guys who said their Mexican help was paying off the Mexican Mafia. They had just found out about it and they were in a fighting mood. I asked what they thought we should do about it and both recommended lynching. I didn't think we could get away with that but having them deported wouldn't work either. I knew of several guys that had been deported and were back at work in a week. We left it at thinking how to deal with these jerks. Our guys worked hard for their money and we had to protect them someway.

The third call was from Detective Capa to tell me my worker had died this morning. I told him I had already found two horsemen that had discovered their help was paying off these crooks. I asked him what he thought we should do about it. He said it was a real problem because these people were all shadow workers. The Justice Department had not decided how their crimes should be handled. They could be deported of course, but that was just a slap on the wrist and they came right back. Putting them in prison wasn't effective because the conditions there were better than many of their lives in Mexico.

I didn't tell him what I was thinking, but that little talk had convinced me we needed to take care of this ourselves. We just needed to find out who they were. It had to be someone connected to the horse business. They would not be able to find these guys otherwise. Offhand I couldn't think Of a Mexican horse trader or stable owner. It had to be someone that visited stables without raising suspicion. Maybe a horse shoer or a hay deliverer or someone like that. If enough guys were on alert for the scout, maybe one of us could turn him up.

I was out of thoroughbred horses and I had good luck with them. The horse auction in Chino was out in the horse country and from time to time one came through the ring there. It was a cattle auction but one night a week they auctioned horses. The man that owned it was one of the principle auctioneers at the horse sales in Keenland Kentucky. I went early to try to talk to the auctioneer thinking he might know of some horses for sale.

I was sitting on a stool at the counter talking to the girl that worked there when he walked in carrying his brief case and his jacket over his arm. He said, "hi Graham, what's doing?"

"I'm just looking for some thoroughbred horses."

"You might be in luck. I've just come from appraising a whole farms worth for the bank. Come on in the office and I'll tell you about them."

He put his brief case on the desk and hung up his jacket. I sat down in the chair facing the desk. He said, "this is really a strange situation. The farm owner came to the bank asking for a loan to buy some horses. Do you know why banks will not loan on horses?"

"I think it's because they don't have any way of knowing the value of them."

He said, "that's correct. You can look at the morning market and know what a cow is worth because they sell by the pound. A horse is all smoke and mirrors. He is worth whatever you can convince the buyer he is worth. In fact, I often quote you on the value of a horse. I overheard you tell a lady right here one night that a horse is worth five cents a pound and how much you love him. The five cents a pound was the killer price at that time. I use that quote often.

What happened with this loan was different from most. The bank wouldn't loan on the horses but they would give him a letter of credit up to the value of his farm. He had one-hundred and fifty-thousand equity in his farm and they gave him a letter of credit for one-hundred and twenty-thousand. He spent the entire amount plus about fifty-thousand of his own money buying horses. He didn't realize that to produce a horse to marketable age took two to three years. He had spent all of his own money and had nothing left to operate the farm for that two or three years.

The poor guy is three months in arrears on his bank loan. The bank doesn't want to foreclose on his farm so they hired me to go out and appraise the situation. The thing he is not taking into account is the horses or not incumbered and he is free to do whatever he needs to do. I suggested he sell whatever he needs to bring his payment current. I did impress on him that he had paid too much for some of the horses, but he has some pretty decent breeding for California. If you can buy fifty-thousand worth of horses right now it would put him right and you could buy some nice horses worth the money. Are you interested?"

"I am very interested. When could I get a look at their breeding?"

He opened his briefcase and called Joan in and told her to copy these papers front and back and to staple them together. She looked at him with a sour face because there were thirty or forty sets of papers but she left with them.

He said, "I made a rough estimate of what I thought the value might be. I have to act in the interest of the bank because they are paying me but he can't expect you to pay top retail money. There has to be enough left on the table for you to make a profit or you wouldn't do a deal. I will give you a copy of the sheet of my estimates and you can make your own estimates. If it looks good to you, I will make arrangement for you to see the horses tomorrow. The rest is up to you. I can't be a part of the negotiations."

I thanked him and went out and sat on the stool at the counter and waited for Joan to finish making copies. When she finished, I took the papers out to my truck and started going over them. There was a dozen of them that I loved the breeding. There was another dozen that had decent breeding. I was guessing that the better-bred mares would be the last ones he would sell. I concentrated on the dozen with just decent breeding which I felt he might sell. I took the list of prices my friend had estimated and started comparing them to the horses I was thinking on. The prices of this group seemed to range from five to ten-thousand and that is about what I would price them at. The price of the rest of the horses which were below this class were estimated from two-thousand to four-thousand. I had to admit that his estimates were spot on with my thinking. I pulled my bank account up on my cell phone and I had sixty-two-thousand in my checking account. I went in and gave him one of my business cards and told him to call me with the time for my introduction to the owner.

I took a long look at the horses that were in the auction tonight and didn't see anything that I wanted, so I went on home. My wife was reading the newspaper when I walked in and she said, "there is something you should take a look at," and she handed me the paper. She had circled a classified ad for a nineteen fifty-four Corvette for four-thousand dollars. It was being sold by a museum.

"Do you know where this museum is?"

"I looked it up. Do remember the street that dead ends at the entrance to Knotts Berry Farm?"

I said, "yes."

"It's on that street about four or five blocks before you get to Knotts Berry Farm."

"I may have to go and look at some horses tomorrow. If I don't, we will drive over and take a look. I can't imagine why a museum would have a corvette."

I knew the call wouldn't come early. He had served as auctioneer until eleven or twelve and had to oversee the settling up afterwards. On an easy night, he wouldn't get to sleep before one or two in the morning. On a busy night, breakfast at Denny's might be his super.

The call came about eleven o'clock and he told me we had an appointment at ten o'clock the next morning and I should meet him at the auction barn. I assured him that I would be there at nine-thirty.

I told my wife I was going to see the Corvette, and asked her if she wanted to go? She didn't think that was funny, but I did. As it turned out, I wished I really had left her at home.

We walked into the museum and right away spotted the White Corvette. We walked down to look at it and the hood was up so you could view the motor. The sign in front of the car said it was built by Don Prudhomme, and it had a Cadillac engine in it. I walked over and looked to be sure it had a Cadillac. My wife says, "it's not original and we are not buying this car."

"You are right, it's not original. do you know who Don Prudhomme is? This is way better than being original."

"I don't care who he is, we are not buying a modified classic car. Once they have been modified, they are worthless."

While I was trying to think of some way to make her

understand the value of this car, I got on my back to look under the car and saw that the frame had been reinforced to handle the bigger engine. I couldn't tell what the transmission was but the rear end was way bigger than the one that came in it.

"I don't know what you are looking at under there and I don't care, we are not buying this car."

"Honey, you don't understand, this car is worth five times what they are asking for it."

"I do understand. You see this little car with enough engine in it to make it go airborne and you are dying to get behind the wheel. Read my lips, we are not buying this car."

Whoever said it's a man's world, was out of his mind. I actually had tears in my eyes on the way home.

I did get my revenge, sort of. A couple of years later she found a Rolls Royce that had belonged to Dean Martin and I wouldn't buy it for her. I told her it drove like a truck and I wasn't buying it. She really wanted it and she didn't give up as easy as I did but I stuck to my guns. She harassed me until someone else bought it, and she still brings it up once in a while to this day. I counter with the Prudhomme car every time she brings it up.

I was at the auction barn by nine fifteen and he was already there. He said it wasn't very far and we had time to stop for coffee. I followed him in my truck because he didn't intend to stay at the farm. He had coffee and

I had a Dr Pepper. I have never learned to like coffee and believe me you are not born liking coffee. We pulled into the farm at exactly ten o'clock.

His introduction was short and sweet. He pointed at the farm owner and said Clay Roberts and he pointed at me and said Graham Peterson. He said you want to sell a few horses and he wants to buy a few. I will leave you boys to it, and he left.

We shook hands and I said, "I kind of expected a little more introduction than that."

He smiled and said, "I think he doesn't want to get caught in a crossfire here. He is trying to stay at arms-length. Where would you like to start. Would you like to talk breeding or see the horses first?"

"First of all, I need to know if you have prices in mind. I don't have the money to be buying a load of fifty-thousand-dollar mares."

He smiled and said, "I don't own any of those. My horses are more modest than that."

"If I pick out a mare can you give me a price for her right now?"

"I think so. I have a list of my mares and I pretty well know what I have to get for each one."

I hoped that he didn't have a list of what he had paid for each horse and intended to sell them at that price or even worse at a profit. I said, "let's go to the horses first, and if I like something, I will ask you for your price. I have the breeding. The girl in the office copied the papers for me."

We went into a pasture with about twenty mares in it and he said, "this is the horses I am willing to sell. I think I should tell you the name of each horse as we come to her and if you like her, I will give you the price. I have been living with these horses long enough to recognize every one of them."

I said, "fair enough, lead on."

I knew going in that these would be the twenty bottom mares in his heard. I didn't have a problem with that as long as each mare was worth the price, he asked for her. The first mare he named as we came to her was near the bottom and the appraisal sheet valued her at twenty-two hundred. Just to get a feel of how this was going to go I asked, "how much?"

He looked at his sheet and said, "Twenty-five-hundred."

I wrote the amount beside her name and we walked to the next one. He gave me her name and said, "seven-thousand five-hundred."

He gave me her name and she was one that I had on my list to look at and the appraisal was sixty-five hundred. I wrote the asking price and we walked on to the next one.

The name of the next one was on my list to look at and she was a grand looking mare. The appraisal was for nine thousand, and he asked for ten Thousand.

I figured we should find out if there was any reason to continue this operation. I said, "so we don't have to look at these mares more than once I am going to start making offers as we go. I don't know what you were told about me, but I am a horse trader. I don't buy them to keep, I buy them to resell. So far you have been asking me what I can sell them for if I am lucky. Please don't be insulted when I offer you less than you think a mare is worth. I am only offering what I think will leave me enough room to make a profit. For the last two mares together, I will give twelve-thousand."

I saw hurt in his face and I felt sorry for him, but I wasn't going to lose money in this deal just because he had made some bad decisions.

"Let me think about it while we are looking at some more of them."

The next one was not on my list and he said that he had just bought her last week. I didn't believe that under the circumstances but it didn't make any difference where she came from when he asked fifteen-thousand for her.

The next one was on the list for three-thousand and I thought that was high. He asked five.

The next one was on my look at list but she was too small for my taste. The appraisal was for six-thousand and he asked sixty-five hundred. I realized that he was using the appraisal sheet also.

The next mare was the cream of the crop in this bunch. She had perfect confirmation and really good breading. The appraisal was for ten thousand and he asked twelve. I put in a bid for nine thousand and would have paid the ten if he had offered. He said again, let me think about it.

The next two mares were bottom feeders and he asked a thousand above the appraisal. I was about to give up on him when he priced the next mare a thousand under the appraisal. She was on my look at list and I liked her until I saw she had a club foot. The next four horses were in the bottom third and he priced them too high.

We were down to the last few mares and I had bought nothing yet. I wasn't going up and if he wanted to sell something he had to come down. The next mare was on my look at list but she was very thin I stood watching her eat and I could see that she was having trouble chewing. It was obvious that she had a bad tooth cutting her when she chewed her feed. That was a simple problem to fix but he didn't recognize the problem. She was appraised for nine-thousand and he asked seven-thousand. I offered six thousand and he gave me the I'll think about it line.

There were only three mares left and we still had not made a deal on any horse. All three of the mares left were on my look at list and it just so happened that all three were appraised for seven-thousand each. From where we were standing, I could see that all three mares looked good. I asked the names of those three mares over there to make sure they were who I thought they were. They were and I said, "since we have not made a deal yet today, I am going to get the ball rolling by making you an offer of fifteen-thousand for those three mares without even looking at them." He said, "let me think about it. While I discuss this with my wife let's go up to the house and have some lunch."

I didn't know we had walked so far out into the pasture until we had to walk all the way back. We had walked two or three miles all downhill. The walk back was all uphill and I was exhausted when we got back.

He said. "have a seat. My wife was making egg salad when I left and maybe she will share it with us. I'll go check on her."

I knew that he wanted to talk to her in private, which was fine with me. There was a Blood Horse magazine laying on the coffee table. I picked it up and was content to sit there for the next hour if need be.

It was about half an hour before he came in with a tray loaded with egg salad sandwiches. She had plates and glasses for us he set the sandwiches down and went back for a picture of lemon aid. We started to eat and nothing was said about the horses until we had finished. The food was delicious and I told them if they ever got tired of horses, they should open a restaurant.

After lunch he helped her clear the table and both of them came and sat down at the table. She started the conversation by saying, "I understand you have made offers on several of the horses."

"That is correct. I made an offer on seven of them. I would make an offer on more of them but I don't have unlimited funds. That is about all I can afford to buy today."

"We have talked it over in the kitchen and we are close. You have offered forty-two- thousand for the seven horses. If you can make it forty-five thousand, you have a deal."

"I'll help you as much as I can. I'll give forty-four-thousand." The other thousand didn't make much difference, but a thousand dollars was a thousand dollars. There have been days when I would have killed for a thousand dollars. She looked at her husband and he nodded yes and she said, "we have a deal. How do you want to pay for them?"

"I will write you a check right now and it will be two are three days before I can come for them so the check will have time to clear before I move the horses. I have a four-horse trailer so I will have to make two trips. Who do I call when I'm coming up to make sure someone is here?"

"I will give you our number. I am here most all of the time but if I am gone, the phone I am giving you rings in the barn and I will alert our barn man to answer the phone and let you in when you come."

I wrote her a check and asked her for a receipt listing which horses I am buying in case I am dealing with the barn man when I come back.

"I'll do better than that. I'll give you their papers right now." She went off in search of the papers and was back in ten minutes. I checked the papers against the names I had written on my list and everything was good. We parted as friends and I got the impression that the money was going to set them right with the world.

It was three days before I had time to go after the horses. I took the horse with the bad teeth on the first load and I had already talked to a horse shoer that also did teeth. He was waiting at the barn when we pulled in and took care of her right away. When I got back with the second load, he was still there flirting with a couple of the female boarders.

He came over to tell me that the mare's teeth were the worst he had ever seen. He suggested that I have him check her again in a month or so. I paid him and told him the two girls he was fooling with were only sixteen. He said damn, you just can't tell anymore, and got in his truck and drove away.

It was good to have mares to sell again. I was tired and didn't feel like going to the Friday night auction so I went home and perused their papers. Three of the mares had been winners at the racetrack and that always raised their value a little bit. I had a good group of mares and they would make a profit. One or two of them I was tempted to keep and breed myself.

There was a pair of brothers that had an auction up in the north west. One of them had brought a trailer load of horses to the auction here and done very well with them. He was impressed by the action here and ended up buying a small auction out in the country. They must have had a big operation because a week after he bought it, he had fifty head of horses on the grounds. He had brought some people with him and he had hired some people here that were working at other auctions. There was one guy that went everywhere with him we could never figure out what he was supposed to be. He went everywhere with him as if he was a body guard. The new auction owner gave credit pretty easily which is not a good thing with horse traders. They are notoriously bad pay. This guy was also his bill collector. He represented himself as one bad ass mother. But no one had ever seen him fight.

We had a kid who had come down from Salt Lake City that had started hanging around the auctions. He was about twenty-five and a real clean-cut good-looking kid. One night at the big auction which was on Friday night the body guard was trying to throw his weight around and intimidate people. He got in an argument with the kid and the kid punched his lights out. The kid made it look easy and his career as a tough guy was over. He might as well go back up north; he was done here.

Most of these guys were here to try to make a living and fights were rare. I did see one that in a way was comical. It was at the same auction. The guy that rode the saddled horses in the ring was a pretty good cowboy. He was from South Dakota and he and his brother were real cowboys. During the horse sale an older gentleman had come into the ring to watch. He was leaning against the fence right under the auctioneer. He didn't bid and he didn't even look closely at any of the horses. After about an hour the auctioneer, who happened to be the owner leaned over and said, sir would you please leave the sale ring. The guy looked up at him and didn't say a word but he didn't leave. He looked to be about sixty and was on the thin side. I would guess he was five seven, and a hundred and thirty pounds. He kept standing there and the rider was moving the horses around trying to make them look better broke than most of them were. It was a possibility that one of them could run over this guy. After a while the auctioneer leaned over and said sir, there are plenty of seats, would you please leave the sale ring. The guy looked up at him again and said nothing but he did not leave.

When the sale was over, and traders were milling around talking, the guy was still around. The rider was standing there talking to a couple of guys and the owner came over and handed him a twenty-dollar bill and said don't hurt him but go slap the shit out of that old man. He put the bill in his pocket and walked over and slapped the guy hard enough that you could hear it all over the barn. The guy backed up a step and then knocked the rider flat on his ass. He sat there a minute looking a little confused. We were all watching him to see what he would do next. We all expected to see him get up and destroy this little old man. He shook his head a couple of times and hopped up. He walks over to the guy who is just standing there watching him. As soon as he was within reach the man hit him in the face with two little quick left jabs and then unloaded with a right in the gut that bent the rider over on his hands and knees gasping for air. The old guy just backed up and stood there watching to see if he had enough or was going to come back for more. One of the rider's friends came over and said let's go eat I'm hungry and squatted in front of him in case the guy decided to kick him. He finally got his breathing under control and they left.

I walked over to the guy and said, "You fight amateur or professional?"

"Professional ten years."

I said, "I tell all my friends to never start a fight with a stranger. You never know what you are running into."

"That's good advice. You must have fought a little to recognize that I had."

"I tried Golden Gloves two years in high school and realized that I wasn't a fighter. I have molars missing to prove it."

He laughed and walked away with a wave of his hand.

I had breakfast and intended to spend the day looking over the new mares. I had noticed that two or three of them looked kind of shabby. They were going to need a little cleaning up to look their best. Hair clipping in a few places and some hoof trimming. It was nothing serious but it would let them show better.

I was out in the paddock among the mares when my phone rang. It was Hugh Edward, the guy trying to establish a breeding farm out near Thousand Oaks. "What's up?"

"I just had a very strange thing happen to me."

"Tell Me about it."

"I was in Kentucky at a Thoroughbred auction and I found out one of the auctioneers lives here in Southern California. I spoke to him and he gave me his number. I called him yesterday to ask if he knew anyone with Thoroughbred mares for sell. He gave me a phone number and when I called it, I was told you had already bought the mares. How do you stay so tuned in to what's going on in the business?"

"It's easy. You just have to drive two or three hundred miles a day visiting people and asking questions. I listen to more gossip every week than the nosiest busy body in any neighborhood in the world. Sometimes it pays off, but most of the time it is a waste of time."

"Did you get anything I might need?"

"I think there are two or three of these mares that any-one can use. They are a pretty good bunch of young mares. Come by and take a look or give me your email address and I'll send you a copy of their breeding."

"I'm stuck in the city all day with nothing to do, but I can't leave because I am the only one in the office right now. How about I give you my office email and you send them here?"

"That works for me. It will take me a while to scan the papers, but you can expect them in about an hour. I will talk to you after you have looked over the breed-ing."

I went up to the office and started scanning the papers and while I waited for each one to go through the ma-chine, I called a farrier to come by and trim some feet. He said he would be here about two o'clock. When I finished scanning, I emailed Hugh, and then I took a pair of scissors and a pair of hand clippers to the pad-dock to do some tidying up.

Luckily, they were all gentle and allowed me to trim the hair around their fetlocks and around their ears without trying to kill me. I intended to just trim the best three, but once I got started, I went through them all. I was glad that every halter had a brass name tag on it. I would still check them against their papers, but the name tags saved me a lot of time.

Hugh called me again about five o'clock to tell me that he was stuck in after work traffic and wasn't moving very fast. He said he would stop and look at the mares on his way home if he got here before dark. He said he liked the breeding on every one of the mares. Especially the three that were winners. I told him I would hang around the office until dark and if he didn't make it, he could see them tomorrow.

The farrier had just finished the last horse when Hugh drove up to the barn. He saw us at the paddock and walked out where we were. Freddy had loaded his gear in the truck and we were just standing there talking and he drove out when he saw my customer arrive. I think Hugh thought he was someone looking at the mares. I didn't mention who he was, and let him think whatever he wanted to think. It never hurt to have a prospective buyer think someone else might be interested.

I said, "how is everything going with you?"

He was looking over my shoulders at the mares and answered on remote control, "everything is normal with me."

I said, "come on out and look at these mares. Was there any one that you wanted to see first?"

He said, "I would like to look at all of them. I liked the breeding on everyone. I don't know how you manage to put these well-bred mares together. I can't find anyone but you who has any decent mares. It seems that most of the mares in California are very ordinary, with weak breeding."

"People in California are too busy to spend the time it takes to learn about breeding. There is too much going on in their lives. Most have jobs that are time consuming, and too many different kinds of recreation. They are going sailing this weekend and next weekend they are going skiing or ice skating in the mountains.

I have a sometime buyer who has all of the money in the world. Someone gave her my name and she called me up to ask for advice and to buy a few horses for her. She bought what had been a very famous Quarter Horse ranch and bought what had been the Champion two-year old thoroughbred, as a stud prospect. She then proceeded to buy five-hundred-dollar mares to breed to him. She asked me to be the manager of her ranch and I declined the job, but I found her a lady that had been in the horse business for a long time.

That was a mistake. The lady and her girlfriend moved on the ranch and started managing. The problem was that the gay community was really into Arab Horses and as soon as they were really connected with the owner, they started lobbing for her to start investing in Arabs instead of Thoroughbreds. The key thing here is the five-hundred-dollar mares. People that don't study breeding think the mare is not important. I cannot tell you how many times I have people tell me they always buy fillies because if they can't run, they can breed them. Why would you expect a mare that can't run to produce a foal that can run? If you breed failure you most likely are going to produce more failure."

While I am shooting off my mouth about one of my pet peeves, he is looking at the mares. He spent a good hour looking at the mares. I wouldn't care if he took an entire week to look them over. He was not going to find any faults in any one of them. They were a great bunch of young mares.

When he finished looking, he came over and said, "hit me with the bad news. Tell me what they are going to cost me."

I was sort of confused about what he was asking so I said, "which one?"

He said, "I like them all."

I thought oh boy, could I be this lucky? But what I said was, "I tell you what I will do. If you want to negotiate, we have to do it horse by horse. I will give you a whole herd price but I won't negotiate any on that price. If you take the entire group, I will sell them to you for sixty-four-thousand-dollars.

I should tell you I have been considering keeping a couple of them to breed myself. The only reason I don't, is because I have lived with me my whole life, and I know I don't have the patience for breeding. I am too impulsive. Someone would make me an offer I liked and I would sell them. I once went to the race track with six young two-year-olds. I never got one of them to the races. People kept making me offers and I kept selling them. A month ago, I sent four colts to the race track with my exercise rider and had sold them in two weeks. That is a fair price for this group and I have not had time to show them to anyone else yet."

"If you will deliver them Saturday morning, I will meet you at the ranch at ten o'clock and give you a check."

"I think you have bought some nice mares. I'll see you Saturday. I will have the first load there by ten o'clock."

When I pulled in to his place on Saturday, his wife was with him. He introduced me to her and said, "be careful around her right now. She is trying to go vegetarian and it has made her very cranky."

"I tell you what I will do. If you will go out to dinner with me tonight, I will take you to the vegetarian rehabilitation center."

I could see her mouthing the words to herself trying to make sense of it and she said, "I never heard of it. What is that?"

I said, "Ekberg's Stake House. It's the best steak house within several hundred miles."

He laughed, but she didn't, so I decided I should stop with the humor.

I unloaded the second load about one o'clock. We concluded our business and I drove away feeling good. I had made some money and he had received a good bunch of mares for his money.

On the way home a friend called that I hadn't talked to in a year or so. We went through the usual what have you been up to questions before he got down to the reason he called. He asked, "do you know Delta Downs?"

"Sure, I raced there a couple of times years ago. It's in Vinton Louisiana right on the Texas border."

"What would you charge me to haul four horses there for me?"

"Why would you need me to haul horses when you have two or three horse trailers?"

"I am taking ten horses down to race there and I only have a six-horse trailer."

"My first reaction would be to tell you that it is not a place where outsiders can win. The whole jockey colony is controlled by a couple of guys. They decide who is going to win every race. You have to wait your turn to win a race."

"I know that, and that is why I am going. One of those guys is my cousin and he said they need some new blood and for me to come down."

"My question is are we going down together in convoy?"

"Yes, if you can get away by tomorrow."

"If you put all of my gas on your credit card, I will do it for five hundred dollars."

"The horses are at Los Alamitos. Can You meet me there at ten o'clock in the morning? I'm in barn six."

"I will be there. See you then."

Tomorrow was payday for my two wranglers. I would pay them today and take them to the market. I would be back before next payday. I had a couple of other errands to run and a couple of people to call before I left town. other than that, I was ready to go. After I had finished my chores, I packed a bag with enough clothes for a week. I put my bag in the truck and hooked up my trailer. I was ready to go.

I spent a lot of nights at the horse auctions and I normally didn't go to bed until one or two o'clock in the morning. I was used to sleeping until eight or nine. Since I was supposed to meet him at ten and he was about a two-hour drive, I set an alarm. I did it so rarely it took me ten minutes to figure out to set it.

I ate my normal breakfast of cereal and put my little cooler with eight Dr Peppers and a half bag of ice behind the seat and headed out. I hopped he wasn't a weenie that only wanted to drive six or eight hours a day. I liked to drive until I became sleepy and I didn't get sleepy until about midnight. Six or eight-hour days would add an extra day to the trip. I had a pair of walkie talkies that plugged into the cigarette liter so we could communicate on the road.

I pulled into his place at nine-fifteen. I wanted to be early so I could make sure he was on the move. I didn't want to lose half a day while he dinked around. I was pleased to see that he was hooked up and already loading horses. I pulled over beside his rig and while they finished loading horses, I put two bales of his hay in the back of my truck. He asked if that was enough and I put two more bales in. I followed him out of the gate at ten minutes before ten. I keyed the walkie talkie and said it's a good day slugo. I mainly wanted to be sure we were in touch. He came back with a ten-four and everything was good.

We wheeled along at the speed limit and made our first stop for fuel and a sandwich at about two o'clock. We had an argument when we hit the spot where highway ten and highway twenty merged coming west. He wanted to stay on the ten because it went straight into Louisiana, and I wanted to take the twenty because it was a much better highway. He insisted on the ten and admitted later he wished we had taken the twenty. The drive across Louisiana was like running a marathon on a railroad track. It seemed as if it would never end. Miles and miles of nothing but bad road. By the time you finally reached decent highway you had learned to hate the state.

We pulled into Vinton in the middle of the afternoon and as we left the Interstate there was a new little restaurant with a sign that said bacon and eggs two-ninety-five served all day. I made a note to stop there on the way out, that sounded good.

As his guys unloaded the horses, I added up my gas

expenses for the trip down. He had charged my gas on his credit card coming down but I wouldn't have his credit card going back. I had spent two-hundred and eighty dollars on the way down. My gas mileage would be a little better going back without the weight of the horses so I told him I would take two-hundred. He gave me seven-hundred and my walkie talkie. I wished him luck and hit the road.

The trip home didn't take near as long as going. I have always had a peculiar trait. If I get sleepy and take an hour nap, I am good for another four or five hours. By pulling over at rest stops and sleeping an hour or two every few hours, I basically drove straight through.

When I reached home in the early evening, I checked out the barn and when everything looked good, I went to bed. I hadn't gone to bed at eight o'clock very often but I didn't wake up until the phone woke me at seven-thirty in the morning.

It was a friend that had a little stable near Gardenia. He called to tell me the Mexican Mafia had hit his guy last night. His guy had paid them but he had got the licenses plate number of the truck they were driving. I called Detective Capa, and asked him to run the plate for me. He wasn't exactly eager to do that. He didn't want to get involved in this whole thing and I explained that we didn't want him involved. This was one thing we wanted to take care of on our own. He finally agreed to run the plate and said he would call me back.

I asked Jose which one of the guys had done the beating and he said the big guy had done the hitting while the Mexican guy had held him. Detective Capa called me back and gave me a name and address on the truck. I knew who the guy was but I didn't know where he lived.

I had seen a flat leather leaded, sap that the police used to carry, in an antique store a month ago. I went back to see if it was still there. It was, and I bought it. I had a Smith and Western snub nose thirty-eight for which I had a concealed carry permit. I drove out to the address Capa had given me. It was a little frame house on the outskirts of Ontario and there was a white flatbed truck parked in front. I didn't know if he lived alone or not so I left my pistol in my holster.

I knocked, and when he opened the door, I could tell by the look on his face that he was my guy. He backed up a step and I pushed into the house. I didn't see any evidence that he had a roommate. I said, "I think you know why I'm here. Do you want to talk to me or do I have to beat you to death like your friends did to my man?"

He looked as if he was thinking about running for it. I slipped the pistol out of my holster and said, "If you run you die."

He sat down in a chair with a plop as if his legs were too weak to hold him up and said, "what do you want to know?"

"I want to know who the two guys were that beat my guy to death. If you lie to me, I will be back and I won't give you a chance to talk to me the next time."

He gave me the names without hesitation and it made perfect sense. It was the fake tough guy from Idaho and the Mexican guy that had worked at the Friday auction for years and now worked for the same guy that the tough guy worked for. The driver of the white truck also worked for the same guy hauling horses. All three of them worked in the same place and had dreamed this scheme up between themselves.

I called Capa and told him it was two white guys and one Mexican. I wanted to know if he was going to prosecute the two white guys. He started tap dancing, "I already told you this is a very murky situation and I don't know what I can do at this point."

"That is all I wanted to know. If you can't go after them, I think it best that you don't know who they are. I think they call that deniability." I hung up the phone before he had time to tell me what he thought about that.

I looked around the little house and did not see a phone. I asked, "do you have a cell phone?"

He said, "I have one, it's in the truck but the battery is dead. They want more for a new battery than I can buy a new phone for."

"Listen to me very carefully if you tell either one of

them that I was here, I will tell them you ratted them out and stand back to watch them beat you to death. If you don't mention it to them, I will leave you out of the storm that is about to roll over them. Do you understand me?"

He nodded his head yes and I walked out and drove away. I called the two friends that knew for sure that their helpers had been robbed. I told them that the guys would be at Country Auction tonight and asked if they wanted to go with me. One of them said yes and one of them said he and his wife were going to her parents for diner and he couldn't make it.

I picked up Paul and we drove out to the Country Auction. I said, "they won't know who you are and they won't be watching you. You just hang around and watch my back to make sure they don't blind side me. I'll take care of the business."

It was a cool night and I was wearing a light jacket which was perfect because I had a cover for my pistol. I had slipped the sap up the sleeve of my jacket and the elastic around the cuff was just enough to keep it from slipping out. With any sharp move it slid right into my hand. I kept walking through talking to different people and keeping an eye out for tough guy.

I finally saw tough guy on the other side of the ring but I pretended I didn't. There were twenty horses tied outside of the auction ring waiting for their turn to be sold. I drifted down the line looking as if I was going to buy something.

Tough guy saw that I was down in the semi dark by myself and came strolling down like he didn't see me. I dropped the sap into my hand and stopped to look carefully at a horse. He walked up beside me and said, "I don't think you are welcome here."

"I know you don't think, because you don't have anything to think with."

I gave him about ten seconds to understand what I had said and I hit him about a half inch above his ear. His knees buckled and he went down on his hands and knees. Then I really went to work on him. I would hit him in the ear and then back hand him in the face. I didn't hit him hard enough to knock him unconscious but I was breaking the skin with every blow.

I had mashed his nose as flat as a pancake. I had put cuts over both eyes and the blood was running into his eyes. He was going to have two cauliflower ears. I wanted him to remember this night for the rest of his life. He was still aware what was happening to him and he held his hand up to ward off the blows. I said, "is this the hand you used to beat him up?" I reached out a grasped his fingers and bent them back until I heard a loud snap. He let out the deepest moan I have ever heard.

I said, "Listen to me very carefully. If you ever come back to my place, I promise you that you will never leave it. I will bury you in the manure pile where you belong."

I started to walk away and I turned back and said, "I almost forgot you broke some of his ribs," and kicked him as hard as I could in the ribs. He folded up in a fetal position. I said, "tell your amigo that he is next on the list and I am looking forward to it."

I walked back in the auction thinking if super mex was around, I would take care of him tonight also. I looked for him but he wasn't here. I asked one of the guys that worked the ring if he knew where he was and he said he had gone to Idaho with a load of horses. When he gets back would you tell him that Graham was looking for him and to give me a call. He said he would tell him.

I nodded to my partner and we left. No one had found tough guy yet but they would be bringing those horses in soon where he is laying.

The next day I got a call from the auction owner. He said, "my man is in bad shape and as near as I can tell he is saying you did it. You wouldn't do something like this to one of my people, would you?"

I said in a calm voice, "your man made two mistakes that I take offence to. The first mistake was he came to my place and beat one of my people to death. The second mistake was he came after me in the dark to threaten me and tell me that I wasn't welcome at your auction. I don't take threats very well and I hope that's not why you have called me."

"No, that's not why I called you. I wanted to know if it was you and I wanted to know why. I didn't know about your man and I had no idea he came out to threaten you. All of that had nothing to do with me."

"While we are talking about it, I might as well tell you that I'm not through yet. Ruiz was with him and held my guy while tough guy beat him to death. Ruiz has an ass whipping coming and I might get carried away considering the whole thing was his idea. I don't want trouble with you but don't try to protect him. If he comes back to town, he will get at least the same good ass whipping as tough guy."

He said, "I don't have anything to do with this and I won't give you any trouble over it. I would feel the same way in your place. Although I have to say, I will try to keep Ruiz in Idaho because he is a good worker. I am glad we got this cleared up and I'll talk to you later."

Tomorrow I need to go for a load of hay. The delivery charge is more than the cost of the hay, so I haul my own. I have a twenty-four-foot trailer with three axels under it that I haul my hay on. I bring it in and leave the hay on the trailer. When it gets down to less than a ton, I unload the little bit left and go for hay. A load of ten tons lasts from a month to six weeks. I have a metal roofed carport to park my trailer under to protect the hay

I used to buy it in Antelope Valley but when the gas shortage occurred in the early seventies, electricity went off the grid. All of the alfalfa ranches couldn't afford to lift the water to irrigate and they all closed up. I now have to go another fifty miles to Taft. To show how extreme this jump in power bills was I will tell you about a fellow that I had been introduced to in Tehachapi.

He had a car dealership in Los Angeles and decided it was time to retire. He sold his dealership and looking for something to do he bought an apple orchid in Tehachapi. He and his wife were sitting at the kitchen paying bills. He would look at the bill and if it was ok, he would give it to her to write the check. He had looked at past electric bills before he bought the farm. The bills had been running from a thousand to eighteen-hundred. He handed her the bill and said it's for fifteen-hundred. She said you had better look again. It is for fifteen-thousand. He said I knew I was in trouble.

There were probably fifty of those small alfalfa farms that closed up. You drive through that country today and there is nothing to indicate there ever were hay farms there. It is just high desert like the rest of the surrounding landscape. It is a shame because it was the most beautiful hay I have ever seen.

On the way to get hay I often stop at a friend of mine's farm to visit. He built the neatest horse barn I have ever seen. He dug a footing trench and filled it half full of gravel. He stood rail road cross ties up side by side. He put a plate on the top, and poured cement around the base. He put a metal roof on it and lined the inside walls with plywood. It made a twenty-stall barn strong enough to hold elephants that looked really good. The best part was it cost less than fifteen thousand dollars. He races Quarter Horses so we are not competitors, but I like to stop and see what he is doing from time to time.

The last time I stopped, I kidded him about using an old flip phone. He said that the phone did what it was supposed to do. It let him make phone calls. I told him that the new phones did everything. You could send and receive emails, you could take pictures with it, and you could even watch the races on it if you wanted. He asked why anyone would want to do all of those things on their phone? I told him that you had to keep up with the new technology of the world, the stone age didn't end from lack of stone. He looked at me as if I had lost my mind, so I dropped the subject. I told him he needed to get out more and went on my way.

I had a lady call me about a horse that she had bought for her daughter. Her daughter was only thirteen and the horse they had bought was too high strung for her. I invited them to come over and look through my horses. If they found something they liked, we could maybe make some kind of trade. They looked at horses for the whole weekend. She road nine different horses before she settled on one that she liked. I went to her place to look at her horse. Since she was a good-looking mare, I took two hundred and traded with her. When I loaded her horse to bring him back, he swung his head and hit me in the forehead with his head. The buckle on the halter cut a gash that bled pretty good. I don't know why, but a forehead always seems to bleed a lot. When we came back to the barn, I saddled him to see what the problem was. The horse was on his toes trying to run away. A lot of miles cured that problem and he became a nice horse.

No one mentioned the cut until I went to the Friday night horse auction. I was standing with several friends just talking when one of them said, "what's with the cut on your forehead?"

I said, "I helped a little old lady across the street and she hit me with her cane."

"Why would she do that?"

"She didn't want to cross the street."

Everyone groaned and the group broke up. Everyone went their own way. Gossip time was over and they went back to thinking about doing some business.

Over the years I had a lot of calls about buying horses from people that had daughters going off to college. I probably bought twenty or thirty horse for that reason and passed on another twenty or thirty because they wanted too much for their horse. One of the complications of those deals was that they wanted you to also buy their tack. They couldn't understand why you only offered two hundred for a saddle they paid five hundred for. Saddles didn't usually have a lot of wear on them but bridles were a different matter. Very often the deal breaker was offering one hundred for a bridal they had paid three hundred for. They usually showed a lot of wear and might not sell for the hundred I was offering. They would decide that I was not being honest with them and back out of the whole sale.

One of the things that was profitable for me was selling horse trailers. Oklahoma City has several large horse trailer manufactures. Since I pass through there five or six times a year, I decided to find one of the manufactures that would sell me trailers at wholesale, dealer price. It saved me a lot of fuel by being without a trailer all the way to Oklahoma, and I would make a few bucks by selling the trailer after I came back to Los Angeles. I was turned down by three of the companies before I found one that would sell to me. I created a market for the trailers and guys began to put in orders. They would tell me the type and color they wanted. I could call ahead and they would have it waiting for me. It was an easy four or five hundred without any extra work.

One time I picked up a trailer on my way to the horse auction in Fort Smith Arkansas. A big trader came to the sale with three semi loads of horses. He protected his horses with high prices and drove up the price of all of the horses. The horses were selling for more than I could sell them for and I didn't by a single horse. I was talking to some guys in the parking lot and one of them asked about my trailer. It was obvious that it was brand new and he was curious about it. Before we were finished, I had sold him the trailer and called the manufacture to have one just like it ready for me to pick up on the way back. It was a popular type and color so there was no problem with them having another one for me.

When I came home my wife said. "let's go on a vacation."

I said, "what are you talking about? We live on a vacation."

She said, "I know, but you are always trying to make a buck and it makes it not a real vacation. Remember the time we rented a canoe and drifted down the Colorado River to Yuma. That was one of the best trips we ever took. Wouldn't it be fun to take our canoe and do it again?"

"Sure, it would be fun. When are you wanting to go?"

"How about next week?"

"I think the only thing we will need, is a new dome tent and a new air mattress. The last time I looked at them in the storage shed they looked poorly. It is not likely to rain this time of year. But if it does, I don't intend to sleep in a puddle. I also don't think I would enjoy sleeping on the ground because my mattress went flat. I'll pick those up tomorrow. You can start collecting all of our camping gear in case there is something else we need."

I went to a sporting goods store for the tent and mattress. I could probably buy them at Walmart for half the price but I felt that something like this might be a little better quality at a specialty store.

I have an Old Town canoe and I put it on a trailer. I had first tried a ladder rack but even though they claim the canoe only weighs seventy pounds, it was a strain to get it up on the rack. Either they are fudging their weight claim or I am not as strong as I used to be. I bought a little john boat trailer and modified it slightly. It works great for the canoe.

We got all tied on and left Monday morning. My wife drove the pickup and I followed on my Gold Wing. We went to the canoe rental place in Needles and I made a deal with the guy to launch the canoe from there, and to leave my motorcycle for a few days. We unloaded the canoe and put all of our gear in it, and drove on to Yuma. I made a deal with the guy in Yuma to leave my truck and trailer for a few days. We went back to Needles on the motorcycle and launched the canoe.

We only had three or four hours of daylight left, so we weren't going to get far before we had to set up camp. I was amazed at the growth of homes. It had been twenty plus years since we had made this trip but I had not expected this many homes to be along the river. In the last trip we had not seen more than a dozen homes on the entire seventy-mile trip. The town of Needles stretched ten miles along the river which was different. We had barely passed the last of the houses when we found a place to make camp.

We camped on a sand bar that first night. It was a nice size and in the middle of the river so we didn't have to worry about small critters. We set the tent up and blew up the mattress before we made some hot dogs.

In the morning, the sun was shining bight and not a cloud in the sky. You knew it was going to be a hot day. The great thing about a river trip was the water. When you got hot, you slipped over the side and let the water cool you off. You were dry in a half hour and thinking about going in again. We had been underway for about three hours before we saw the first horses. It was a small band of three horses and three burros. There was a mule with them and I don't remember ever seeing a wild mule before. It made me wonder how that came about. They were standing in the shade of a couple of scrub trees with a couple of them laying down. They kept an eye on us but they didn't seem worried.

It was late afternoon before we saw another group. It was several hours later but we hadn't gone that far. The thing about drifting is you only paddle enough to keep your canoe straight, so you aren't going very fast. This was a larger group and there were several mares with babies. The babies were curious and watched us closely. The older horses didn't seem to care and barely looked at us. The horses looked to be in excellent condition. I'm sure that being this close to the river makes for a good life for them. This group had about a dozen and they all were fat and healthy looking.

During the next few days we saw small groups of horses of four or five twice more. We saw wild cats twice but one of them was big enough that he might have been a panther. We saw wild hogs drinking out of the river and we saw a cow standing shoulder deep in the river. I say it was a cow but it could have been a steer. Whichever it was, it was alone.

We reached the dam at Yuma at noon on the sixth day. I have bought horses from the guys at the feedlot there, and while I was so close, I called them to ask if they had anything I might could use. The manager didn't have anything right now that he wanted to sell. He told me that he had a guy who had stopped a couple of times that claimed he had a dozen two and three-year old geldings. He says they are broke and ready to go. The next time I hear from him, I will give him your number.

We put the canoe on the trailer and went back to Needles to pick up my motorcycle. I asked my wife if she had enough vacation. She said it had been fun and we should do it again next year. I didn't comment on that, but I was glad I was going to be riding behind her on the motorcycle. I couldn't be pressured into something I wasn't sure I wanted to do.

The next morning, I was sitting in my office thinking

about finding some horses to buy. You can't sell them if you don't have them. I had sixty head at summer camp, but they wouldn't be for sale until the camps closed down at the end of summer.

Besides, those were just horses. What I need, are some high-grade horses. I need to find some registered Thoroughbred or Quarter Horses. I don't have a single nice horse on the place. To make matters worse, they called me this morning from the Will Rogers polo grounds and told me they needed four or five young polo prospects. In the last few years, I have sold them a dozen polo ponies. I would hate for them to buy from someone else because I don't have anything to sell them.

I called the Yuma feed lot again and asked the manager if any of the guys working the feedlot might know this guy, that had the young horses to sell.

He said hold on a second and I'll ask them. He came back in more like ten minutes, and told me his name was Bill Root, and he had a place down by the river called the River Ranch. I called information, and they did not have a listing for Bill Root or River Ranch. I decided that since I wasn't doing anything else, I would just take a drive down there and see if I could find him.

I drove to Needles and turned South toward Yuma. I needed to drive the entire distance on the river road because I had no idea how far from Yuma his place was. It was a good thing I did. The ranch was closer to Needles than Yuma. He had a small hand painted sign with the River Ranch name on it. The drive was dirt and it looked long and dusty. There were no buildings in sight even though I could see a mile or so down the drive. I turned down toward the drive and drove slowly in case the house was set back from the road along here somewhere.

It was at least a mile before I came up to the house and barns. Actually, the place was neat and clean. There were two big barns with corrals beside them, and other things you would expect on a horse farm. There was a round pen and a hot walker machine. The house looked small but I didn't see any evidence of a family. It would be large enough for one or two people. There was a pickup parked back by the second barn and I drove on back there. When I pulled up beside his truck he came out of the barn.

He looked like a thousand other cowboys I had seen around the country. Boots and jeans with a western shirt and a cowboy hat. He was slim and solid looking and could be anywhere from fifty to seventy. He moved like fifty and looked seventy.

I climbed out and went to meet him saying, "are you Mr. Root?"

"I am, what can I do for you?"

"I have been told that you have some young horses for sale."

"Are you looking for registered horses or just ranch stock?"

"I am interested in anything with hair and hooves."

"I have six three-year old registered Quarter Horse geldings. I have four ranch stock geldings and I have two registered Thoroughbred mares. They are both seven years old. What would you like to see?"

"How old are the four ranch stock geldings"

"All four of them are three."

"What are you doing with Thoroughbred mares?"

"I was trying to breed some Quarter Horse racing stock, but it turned out to be too much trouble. I have two half Quarter fillies that are yearlings. I will almost give them to you."

"Let's start with the registered geldings first."

He walked to the front barn and as we walked, he said, "I was just about to put them on the walker. I will put them out and let you watch them walk."

The hot walker was between the two barns as was the round pen. He brought the horses out one at a time and latched them on the walker. It was only a four-horse walker so this was going to be a slow job. When he had all four on the walker. I began watching carefully. All of the horses were nicely made. They were in good flesh and all had nice heads and good hind quarters. After I had watched them walk for twenty minutes, I had him stop the walker to give me a chance to walk around the horses. I needed to be able to stand in front to check the straightness of their legs.

"I have not seen anything to scare me off yet, maybe the price will do that. How much do you have to get for these four?"

"If you only take one or two of them the price is fifteen hundred each. If you take all six, I will take six thousand for the group."

"If the other two are the same quality and looks, I will take all six."

"It's going to take me a while to change the horses. The two Thoroughbred mares are in that corral by the back barn. Why don't you go look them over?"

I walked back and spent some time with the mares. They both had good conformation, but the value of the mares would depend on their breeding. Until I had looked at the papers, they were not worth very much.

In the corral by the front were what I was sure were the two yearling fillies. I walked on up to take a look at them. They were both acceptable, but one of them was nice enough to be shown in a halter class. She was a beauty with lots of muscle where it was supposed to be.

I heard the walker start again and I walked around to look at the other two horses. They were as nice as the other four. After he stopped the walker for me to look them over, I told him I would take all six of them.

"I asked the price on the Thoroughbred mares and told him that the value of them was strictly in the breeding. I couldn't estimate the price I would pay until I had seen the papers."

He said, "I have to get two thousand each, and I have the papers in the office." He went down to the front of the barn where his office must be, and came back with all of the papers. He handed me the papers on the mares and I scanned the breeding. The one mare had no breeding at all. She was out of Arizona by horse trailer. The other mare was a homerun. She was a granddaughter of Rex Ellsworth's good stud Khaled, and had won five races as a three-year old. I don't know how he had been able to buy this mare and I wasn't going to ask him. The no breeding mare was worth four or five hundred dollars, but this mare was worth at least five thousand and probably more. I took them both for the four thousand.

I said, "the only things left to see, are the ranch stock horses." He took me to the back barn and took the horses out of their stalls one at a time. I was thinking to myself that the reason he was so thin and trim was from cleaning all of these stalls every day. No wonder he didn't get to town very often.

He asked four hundred each and that was about what I could sell them for.

I said, "I tell you what I will do. That is all I could get for them, but I will buy them if you throw in the two yearling fillies."

"I was only kidding when I said I would give them to you."

"That isn't giving them to me. The four horses are worth to me about two hundred and fifty each and the fillies are worth about two hundred each. The twelve hundred is what they are worth to me and it gets them off your feed. I have met your asking price on every horse so far. I need to get a little something in this deal."

There were half a dozen other horses in this barn and I assumed these were his own horses. It's hard to work live stock without horses. Raising cattle or horses take horses to handle them.

He shuffled his feet and gazed off in the distance, but he finally said he would take that for all of the horses. I told him I would be back in the morning and I would bring cash. I asked him to write a bill of sale for me, and of course sign off on the registration papers.

I went by the Bank and took out some cash for in the morning. I had a four horse-trailer and a six-horse trailer. No matter how I did the hauling, it was going to take three trips. I called the manager of the Polo Grounds and asked him when would be a good time to show him some horses? He said he wouldn't be available to look at them until three o'clock in the after-noon. I told him I had six registered Quarter Horse geldings for fifteen hundred each, or four unregistered geldings for eight hundred each. Which did he want me to bring? He knew I had a six-horse trailer and he said bring the four unregistered geldings, and two of the registered ones.

I was on the road to the River Ranch at six in the morning. I needed to make two loads by three o'clock. I hoped the loading went smooth or I wouldn't make it. I handed the money to Bill and told him to count it while I was hauling. Bill was a good horse handler and we loaded the Thoroughbred mares and four of the Quarter Horse geldings without any trouble. I took them back to my place. I put them away and went back to the River Ranch for another load. I loaded the other two Quarter Horse Geldings and the four unregistered geldings. I pulled into Will Rogers Polo Grounds at three-fifteen. I pulled on back to the barn and the manager was taking some things out of his car. I think he had just arrived.

I unloaded the four unregistered ones first and Jake looked them over carefully. He asked if I would take six-hundred apiece for them. I told him I was short of nice horses and couldn't let them go for six. After a little back and forth between us I agreed to take seven-hundred apiece.

I unloaded the two registered geldings. I saw the lights go on in his eyes and knew he liked them. He asked if they were all as nice as these two, and I told him they looked like they were all out of the same litter. He said that is a little high for my clients. I laughed and told him some of his people would run a bar tab tonight higher than that. I finally agreed to take a hundred a horse less, if he took them all. He wrote me a check for everything, and I gave him the papers. I went back and loaded the other four. He had shown me the stalls to put them in if he was gone when I got back. I was pretty sure he left right behind me and he knew he wouldn't be here when I got back. My stall cleaner helped me load the horses and I was back before dark. I put the horses in the stalls he had pointed out, and went home feeling that it had been a good day.

In the morning, I changed over to my four-horse trailer and went after the two fillies. I came back and turned them out in one of the big paddocks and they went wild. They were running and bucking and playing tag. I was a little concerned that they might hurt themselves. They were having too much fun. I noticed people driving by were slowing down to watch them. They were putting on quite a show.

I called my guy that was developing a ranch in Thousand Oaks, and asked if he was interested in the Khaled granddaughter. When I told him that she had won five races, he said he would be by after work. I priced her at eight thousand. I went on line to look at her family and made myself sick. A full sister to this mare had produced a colt that had won over three hundred thousand. I had priced her too cheap. She was worth three times that amount. I will never price a mare again before I have looked her up. The guy came by, and of course he bought her. He told me he would leave the check with his wife tomorrow, and I could pick it up when I delivered the mare. I had just left ten or fifteen thousand laying on the table. I told him that he was lucky I had priced her before I looked her up. I even told him about her full sister.

I took the other mare to the Friday night auction and she sold for four hundred and twenty-five dollars. That is about what I thought she was worth. This had been a profitable couple of days. I had no idea about what to do with the two fillies. I don't know why I bought them. There was plenty of grass in their paddock so they weren't going to cost me a lot of money. I would take some time to think about it.

I received a call from a guy that was being transferred to Maine by his company. He wanted a price for my hauling his family's four horses to Maine. I told him the normal rate was a dollar per mile, and the trip to Maine was over three thousand miles. He made a low whistle. I said I am not doing anything important right now, and I will do it for twenty-five hundred. He told me he would discuss it with his wife and get back to me.

I wanted to drive by and see a friend of mine who has a rental stable not too far away. I have been told he has final stage lung cancer. It is just him and his adult daughter. I have to ask if he needs any help with anything. He and his daughter were out doing chores when I drove up. She went on with her work but he came over to talk.

I asked how he was feeling and he said poorly. I asked

if there was anything, he needed that I could help him with. He said there were couple of things that he would like to sell me. I am going to have an auction and good things won't bring any more than the junk. I have two good McPherson saddles and two good silver mounted bridles. One of the bridles has a Garcia bit I have had for forty years. I would like to get five hundred a piece for the saddles, and you give me what you think the bridles are worth. I asked if I could see the bridles and he took me in his tack room.

I knew he didn't have any insurance and he had been taking treatments for his cancer. The bridles were nice and the Garcia bit was worth a couple of thousand. I have always wanted one but you don't see too many for sale.

I said, "Joe, you know I am not a wealthy man. Could you get along on five thousand for everything."

He said, "you don't have to do that. I would be happy with the three thousand it's worth."

"I tried to buy a Garcia bit about three months ago and the guy turned down three thousand. I will stick with the five."

He said, "I sure do appreciate it Graham."

"You just take care of your-self, and call me if you need anything." I loaded my saddles and bridles and went home feeling very sad and depressed.

I had a second call from the gentleman going to

Maine. He said he had not asked how much room I had for their tack and equipment. I told him the horse trailer had enough storage in front to carry all of the feed and water buckets for the trip. My truck had a shell topper on the bed. That would hold all of their saddles and bridles and miscellaneous equipment. If he had other equipment, he would have to rent a You Haul trailer to pull behind his car. He said he would let me know when we were going to leave in a couple of hours.

He called me back in about an hour and said the family was going to leave tomorrow. He would like to load me up and get me on the road in the morning. I told him I would be there at eight in the morning.

I went home and told my wife to pack us up for a six or seven-day trip, we were going to Maine in the morning. The family had a home in Rolling Hills with a barn behind the house. There was no way to drive back to the barn. We had to carry everything out to the street. It took us over two hours to get loaded. He didn't have but one bale of hay left. I had to go by the feed store to buy a couple more. It was nearly noon before we were actually on the road.

When I am on the road with horses, I stop every three hours to water the horses and let them pee. If they absolutely have to, they will pee while you are moving but they don't like to. You can tell that by the fact they all pee when you stop. I keep a hay net in front of them all the time so they can snack whenever they feel like it.

Because I stop so often, it took us three days to get there. The family wasn't there yet and I called him on his cell for instructions on putting the horses away. He said he was less than a hundred miles and would be here in under two hours. I had everything unloaded and put away by the time he came driving in. I could tell he didn't drive much. He looked exhausted. He gave me a check and I went on my way.

While we were coming, my wife said she would like to go to Prince Edward Island. We had been to Nova Scotia but we didn't go across to the island. We had been on a motorcycle trip that time, and it was on the verge of being cold. We wanted to head for a warmer place. I found a place that stored boats and motor-homes for twenty-five dollars a month. I left the horse trailer and told the guy to not bury it, so I couldn't get it out. We were going to only be two or three days, but I wasn't going to haggle over twenty-five dollars. I didn't want to pull it to Prince Edward Island and back.

The trip had a surprise in store for us. We drove through Nova Scotia to the Confederation Bridge to the Island. It was a long bridge and I marked my odometer to check the length. It was eight miles across and I couldn't believe they didn't charge a toll. We drove around for three or four hours and had a bite to eat. It didn't have any special interest for us and we started home. When we came back to the bridge, the surprise was, there was a forty-one fifty charge to get off the Island. They had a bank of machines to accept your credit card. There was no live person, in case you wanted to argue about it. It was the ultimate tourist trap.

We picked up our trailer and went on home. I drove until I was sleepy and my wife would take over for an hour or so while I slept. We drove straight through and made it in two days. My wife hates to travel that way, and doesn't go with me much because I do it often.

I didn't have much going on and I had started playing with the fillies. I had started giving them grain and after a few days they would come when they saw me with the grain bucket. After another few days I was able to catch them when they came. I had started ground driving them and they were coming along pretty good. One day I was out in the paddock with them and I noticed a white car parked across the street. It had dark tinted windows and I couldn't tell who was in it. The window was down a couple of inches and whoever was in the car smoked. It came out at the top of the window. I assumed it was someone watching me fool around with the fillies.

He had watched for about an hour before he drove away. I thought he had driven away, but he came around to the front gate and drove in. He drove back to the paddock where I was with the horses. I thought maybe I had a prospect for one of the fillies.

That thought faded as soon as he got out of the car. It was Ruiz, the Mexican guy that had been in on the killing of my worker. He was carrying a machete, and as he came through the gate. He said, "I heard you were looking for me to whip my ass. You have found me, and I am going to cut your head off."

I said, "you are one dumb son-of-a -bitch. You bring a machete to a gun fight." I shot him twice in the center of his chest. He sat down on his butt and looked at me as if to say I don't believe this. He tried to say something but no sound came out. He finally leaned sideways and fell over. His eyes were open but I was sure he was dead. I wear my shirts untucked all of the time and he never realized that I had a thirty-eight on my belt. I had carried it for years.

I called the Van Nuys Police station and asked for Detective Capa. When he came on the line, I told him, "I have just killed the Mexican that was behind the killing of my guy. I think you need to come over here to the farm and bring the Coroner."

"What was he doing at your farm?"

"He came with a machete and told me he was going to cut my head off."

"Don't touch him. I'll be right over."

That's a half hour drive and he was there in fifteen minutes. I had stayed with the body to make sure the fillies didn't nose around and move him or step on him. As sure as they heard the gun shots my two workers had disappeared. He drove up to the barn and I whistled and waved at him. He saw me and drove on over to the paddock. I showed him the body and he looked him over carefully and took pictures of him.

He said, "he didn't want to touch him until the Coroner arrived. He asked me for my gun and asked if I had a carry permit?"

I told him, "I have a permit that I have had a long time."

"Why does a guy raising horses need to carry a gun?"

"I don't raise horses. I buy and sell them. When you buy horses from people that don't know you, they don't like to take a check. I am often carrying five to twenty thousand dollars in cash. A couple of weeks ago I took forty-thousand out to Ontario, to pay for a group of Thoroughbreds I was buying. Until now, I have never needed a gun but I always felt more comfortable with it. I am sure glad I had it today."

The Coroner's van pulled in and Capa waived at him. He pulled back to the paddock and came in to look at the body. He took a temperature of the body and asked how long he had been dead? When I told him less than an hour, he nodded his head at the detective. He asked what kind of gun? I told him it was a thirty-eight. He asked what kind of bullets I had in it? I told him that a police officer had told me to use critical defense bullets. He said if I hit them in the torso with that bullet, they were going to die.

Detective Capa said, "we should go to your office while the Coroner finishes his business."

We walked up to the office and he asked, "when is the last time you saw Ruiz before today?"

"I don't really know. I haven't seen him in months. I have never spoke to him, but I would see him from time to time around the auction where he worked. He changed auctions, and I don't go to the new auction he works for. I went out there about a month ago and beat the crap out of his partner, but he wasn't there. I left a message that I was looking for him."

"Are you sure he was one of the guys that killed your employee?"

"One hundred percent. I talked to the guy that drove the truck for them. The whole thing was the brain storm of Ruiz, and he held my man while the other guy beat him to death. I don't really think they intended to kill him, but they did."

"Tell me exactly what happened, and what was said today."

"I was training a little on two babies in the paddock when I noticed this car parked across the street. I couldn't see who was in it because the windows were tinted so dark. I knew there was someone in the car because he was smoking and I could see the smoke coming out at a little gap at the top of the window. He finally started the car and drove around and came through the ranch to the paddock. He came out of the car with a machete in his hand and told me he heard I was looking for him, and he was going to cut my head off. He started for me and I shot him."

"Where are your stall cleaners?"

"I honestly don't know. I don't know if they took off when they saw him, or when I shot him. I don't know where they went, or if they will be back."

"I have your testimony on my recorder and I will have one of the girls type it up. After they fire your gun and check it out, I will bring it back and I will bring the typed statement for you to sign. I don't see any problem with this, and unless the boss doesn't like something about it, I would say it's over."

I called the guy Ruiz worked for and whoever answered the phone went to get him. When he came on the phone I said, "I guess you didn't believe me when I told you to keep Ruiz in Idaho. If you are interested in giving him a decent burial, he is at the Coroners in Van Nuys. I am finished with him."

He said, "you are kidding, right?"

"The white car he was driving is at my place. If it belongs to you, send someone to pick it up. Otherwise, I will have it impounded."

He said, "I guess you are not kidding. The car doesn't belong to me. Do whatever you like with it." He hung up the phone, and I figured I would have to steer clear of him. Mormons have been known to do a little slaying of Gentiles on their own.

 I couldn't wait for tomorrow to come. I wanted it to be back to business as usual. It was near two weeks before Detective Capa brought me the statement to sign. He also brought my gun, which made me feel more comfortable. I had never realized how much having a gun on my hip boosted my confidence. He told me the case was closed and I was officially cleared of any fault.

I had spent the last ten days calling around looking for horses. You can't sell them if you don't have them. Out of maybe a hundred calls, I had bought two horses and they had cost me near what they were worth. I wasn't going to get rich from either one of them. It was clear to me that the fresh horses had dried up around here, and I had to go out of town to find something to sell. The only thing I had sold since the shooting was the two fillies. A guy from Semi Valley that had driven by a few times, and saw me out playing with them, stopped to see if they were for sale. I asked for four hundred each, and sold them for three hundred apiece. He was looking for future barrel racing prospects. They both looked like they were built for speed. I told him I just wasn't in the keeping business.

The Fort Smith Auction was next week. I called the owner and asked if he had any prior idea of what was coming. He told me he had a lot of guys feeling him out about coming, and he was expecting a big turnout. He said that Herman had ruined the last sale with all of his overpriced horses. He was going to make sure that never happened again. He said because he was bringing so many horses, he had made a deal to not charge a pass out fee for the horses he didn't sell. How was I to know he wasn't going to sell any of them. It wiped out the entire auction. Because of him I have made a new rule that I will only accept a maximum of twenty horse from any one guy. Everyone pays pass out fees. I lost money on the last sale and that is not going to happen again.

I could write a check for anything I bought at the auction but I took twenty thousand cash in case I bought from private people along the way.

The hotel I booked in had a bar downstairs. I saw a couple of horse traders I knew in the bar but I didn't go in. Arkansas had a very peculiar law. A bar could not sell mixed drinks, but a person could bring their own bottle and the bar would sell the mixings. They called it a set up. I don't know what the state thought they were accomplishing with this silly law. The bottom line was the guys were getting much drunker than normal, because they felt obligated to drink their entire bottle every time.

 I went to bed early, and was at the auction barn early. I would know some of the traders, but the ones I didn't know, I wanted to watch come in. The quality of their rigs and how the men that worked for them looked, told you a lot about the trader.

There were horses of every type and color. There were

a lot of horses I could use, but the deciding factor was price. I have a good idea of what I can sell a horse for, and I restrict the purchase price to a level that leaves some profit. No matter how much I like a horse, there has to be a profit in him or I don't buy.

I spent a lot of time talking to people. I was always fishing for new suppliers of saddle horses or Thoroughbred mares. I actually would buy anything I saw a profit in. I was pulling a new horse trailer I had picked up in Oklahoma City that I would sell when I got home.

I talked to one fellow that had brought two Thoroughbred mares to sell, but their breeding was subpar. Unless they were super cheap, I would pass. I met a lot of new people anytime I went to a large auction. Most of them were on a small scale and not much help for me. But every now and then you met someone that knowing was an asset. They were prospective customers or suppliers. Either one was going to make money for me. Some of them just made good friends.

The auction started at noon and I was ringside. I was conflicted about how many horses I should buy. I had talked to a semi driver and found out I couldn't use them because they didn't water the horses. They drove straight through. That almost guaranteed that the horses would get sick. I had talked to a van line that hauled race horses. They fed and watered them but they wanted three hundred a horse. I had picked up a six-horse trailer and it looked like that was all

I could buy. I was going to need to be very selective. Only the best would pay their way.

I had not bought a single horse in three hours and the hard seat was killing me. I got up to stretch and go to the rest room. When I came out of the restroom I walked outside. I was just moving around a little and a really fancy horse trailer pulled in the yard. I recognized it as belonging to Barbara from Texas. I walked over to see if she was aboard. She was just climbing down from the cab when I walked up.

"What brings you to a sale like this?"

"I have been ordered to sell some of my mares, and this is the only place available fight now."

"How many do you have on the van?"

"I have a full load of six."

"You know they are not going to bring anywhere near what they are worth here."

"I know that, but my dad is on the war path and said they must be sold now."

"How is the breeding on them?"

"The breeding is too good for here but I have no choice."

"What do you think they are going to bring here?"

"I am afraid they are going to bring less than a thousand a head."

"Would you sell them to me right now, for three thousand each?"

"You haven't even seen them."

"I trust you that they are all nice mares." "You bet your ass I will sell them to you. How are we going to do this?"

"You passed the fair grounds on the way into town. Take the van over there and I will meet you. We can change the horses there." Barbara climbed back in the cab and away they went.

A guy walking by said, "what was that all about?"

"They were lost. They were supposed to meet someone at the fair grounds and they missed it." I walked back into the sale ring just to be seen by the owner. I hung around for about ten minutes and sneaked out and went to the fair grounds.

They already had three of the horses unloaded and I started loading them into my trailer. When we were finished, I wrote her a check and she gave me the papers. She had three bales of hay on her van which she gave me. While I was filling the hay nets, she had her guy water the horses. When I was ready to go, I told her to call me if she had to sell more of her mares. I told her if the auction company happened to call her about the horses, to tell them she had sold them to me over the phone and was just delivering them to me. She thanked me for helping her out, and I got on the road. I liked every one of the mares and went home happy.

With six horses to feed and water every three hours, and stops for sleeping, it took me three days to get home. I was ready to be home by the time I drove in the drive way. The horses all shipped good and were ready to be home also. When I turned them out in the paddock, every one of them rolled in the grass. They found the water trough and then went to grazing.

I did almost the same thing. I had a shower and went to bed at three in the afternoon and didn't wake up until seven in the morning. I was tired.

In the morning I checked to make sure everything was good with the ranch. Then I went in the office and started going through the breeding on the new mares. All but one of them had over the top pedigrees. The one that had a weak pedigree on her dam's side had produced two earners of note. One has won over two-hundred thousand and the other one has won over a hundred thousand and is still on the track. She has a little age on her. She is nine, but you would expect another four or five years of production with no problems.

 I was satisfied with my purchase, and felt sure it was a profitable deal. I would give them a few days to relax and make sure none became sick. I didn't start trying to sell a horse until I was sure they weren't going to get sick. You only get one shot selling a horse. If a buyer comes to look at a horse and he is snotting, he doesn't come back.

I was out in front of the barn roping the top of a fence post. I am not a roper and have never roped a steer in my life, but when I'm bored, I'm hell on them fence posts. An old Chevrolet truck, a forty-eight or forty-nine came driving in. The driver had been here before. He knew where he was going and came right to the office.

I was waiting to see who was driving. A big six-foot four cowboy that I hadn't seen for ten years or so popped out with a wide smile on his face. I said, "I thought you were in jail for stealing horses. Where have you been?"

He said, "I fell into a job as ranch foreman for a cattle ranch over near Wickenburg."

"What did you do? Sell all the cows and run off with the money. It must have been a lot of money, or you wouldn't be driving that fancy five-hundred-dollar truck."

"The owner up and died a month ago before I could steal the money. I have had more than I need of trying to push cattle around on a sage brush ranch. I 'm going to try to start a hay business. There is a farmer over on the Colorado River, that has twenty miles of the prettiest Alfalfa Hay you ever saw. I am over here trying to buy a truck and trailer, and trying to pick up some of the dairy business. I have a couple of bales in the back of my truck. Take a look at this hay."

I walked over and looked at his hay. He was right, it

was beautiful hay. There is no finer hay than desert raised Alfalfa. I was comfortable with my hay source and don't buy enough at one time to be a customer for him. I told him that and he understood that I didn't have a need for twenty-ton loads.

I said, "I'm not a good candidate for your hay, but I might help you on your truck. There is a guy I use sometimes for odd jobs, that works for a guy that has been trucking. For the last ten years he has driven a one-ton truck with a twenty-foot trailer. He has kept it busy and made a decent living with it. About six or eight months ago, he bought a semi-tractor. I don't know why he felt the need to step up, but he did. Two weeks ago, he had a heart attack and died. You might make a deal with the widow to take over the payments on the truck. She certainly has no use for the truck. I'll get his phone number for you. Give me your number and I'll call you with her number."

"That would be great. I was in the neighborhood and I wanted to stop and say hello. I have to get a move on if I want to catch the dairymen in the barns at milking time." He gave me his number and drove away. He was one of my best friends once, but he left the country and I haven't seen him in years.

I went in and called James and asked for Ted's phone number. He of course asked why I wanted it, and I told him. He gave me the number reluctantly, as if I had some immoral reason for wanting it. I texted the number to Dean, and was glad to see him back.

I coiled my lariat and put it back in my truck. I had enough practice today.

I went in the office and started looking through my rolodex for Thoroughbred customers. I'm sure I have all of these people on my phone, but I am old school, and like my rolodex better for this kind of search. The first number I called was Earl Scheib. He was a strange guy. He kept himself fortified from the public. I guess he didn't want to be harassed by people that were not satisfied with the paint job his company put on their car. The only place he could be reached was his ranch, and very few of us had that number. He was a kick to talk to. He was loud and crude and every third word was a curse word.

He knew his blood lines, even though he was too cheap to buy good ones. He came on the phone in typical style. "What do you want dickhead?"

"I have just the mare for a cheap skate like you."

"I don't have all day, tell me what you've got."

I gave him the breeding, and told him about her two colts. I told him about Barbara and her plan to get her stud known. I told him that she was half price because she was in foal to an unknown stud. I told him that I didn't want to hear his moaning and groaning, so I had priced her at only six thousand.

He said, "you are getting as slick as our friend the bloodstock agent. I have to check everything you tell me. Give me her name and I will check her out. If everything is as you say we'll talk price. Also give me the name of the unknown stud she is in foal to."

I gave him the two names and he hung up on me. Like I say, he is a strange dude.

I went out in the pasture and took a half dozen pictures of the mare. I know if he likes her, he will ask for pictures. I came in and looked at the pictures. I took the best three and deleted the other three.

It was mid-afternoon when he called me back. I answered the phone and he said, "why haven't you sent me any pictures yet?"

I said, "they are on your phone dummy." He hung up on me again.

He called back in half an hour. "I can't pay six thousand for this mare. The most I will give is four thousand."

"I am sure you are hurting for money, and to help you out I will swallow five hundred. But if you can't afford fifty-five hundred for a producer like this, I will have to look for another customer."

"You are getting more like our crooked friend every day. You probably bought this mare for a thousand dollars."

"You are one insult away from losing this mare. I don't know how you ever get any horses bought."

"Against my better judgement, I am going to buy this mare but don't ever try to sell me another one. I expect you to deliver her in the morning."

"I know why you don't have any girls hanging around like most stables do. You expect them to put out for free, and they have to listen to all of your bullshit. I'll see you in the morning around ten. If you are not going to be there leave the check with someone who will be." He hung up on me again. I considered calling him back so I could hang up on him.

I got up in the morning feeling like I needed to get out and visit people. I made a vow to myself to fill up my trailer with new horses before I came back to the ranch.

I loaded the mare and went to deliver her. When I got to the farm it was locked up like Fort Knox like always. I blew my horn and waited for someone to come and let me in. I pulled back to the barns and unloaded the mare. A groom came and snapped his lead rope on her halter and I took mine off. I turned around and Earl was standing there.

"I didn't know you could walk. I have never seen you out of your office chair. Were you afraid the pictures I sent you, weren't of the mare I was bringing you?"

"Believe it or not, you are one of the few people in this business that I still trust. I need to ask you something. I have twenty horses in training at the race track. When I retire a stud horse, I don't know what to do with him. They aren't of breeding quality. I can't sell them as a saddle horse without castrating them and having someone spend time retraining Them. That cost more than they are worth at that point."

I said, "are you familiar with the Boarder ranch?" He shook his head no. "It is a ranch at the border at Tijuana. The guy that owns The Tijuana Express, owns it. It is almost impossible for the average guy to take a horse across the border from Tijuana to the US. I made the mistake of doing it once. I was six hours getting across the border. I had my trailer steam cleaned three times before it was clean enough for the border guards.

The Tijuana Express has some kind of deal worked out with them and they don't bother him. He goes back and forth two or three times a day. What people do, is leave their horse at the Border Ranch and The Tijuana Express takes them across. When they are coming out, he brings them across and leaves them at the Border Ranch. The problem with that is, if a horse can't win at the Tijuana track, it can't win anywhere in the states. A lot of them are never picked up. I have a deal with him for several years. When he has five or six of them, he calls me and I go pick them up. I take whatever he has even if they are crippled, for a flat rate of one hundred dollars. I don't make much money off of the deal. If I pick up six horses, I average two that are straight enough to pay for the load. I do it mainly as a service to him. He knows every person in California that is in the horse business. From time to time he has given me leads that made money."

"Would you be willing to do the same deal with me?"

"I guess I will, but I can't come out here for one or two horses. I will put a minimum of four horses before I will come."

"We have a deal, and I have five to go right now. I will go write you a check for five-thousand and give you five sets of papers."

He turned to his groom and spoke in Spanish. Who then went, I assumed, to get the horses. He was the only one there, I guess. He brought them one at a time. I loaded them without any trouble. They were all well-schooled. I could see right away this was going to be a higher quality of horses than I was getting from Tijuana. This might prove to be profitable. He sent the check and papers out to me with a maid. I had to bite my tongue to keep from sending a message back to the arrogant prick.

I brought them to the ranch and looked each one over as I took them off the trailer. All five were still studs and had to be put in stalls to keep them separated.

I don't use veterinary services that often, but I had tried three or four over the years. I had never found the one who I thought knew as much about a horse as I did. They take them into school and teach them how to give injections, and how to suture a wound and things of that sort. What they don't realize is that a guy has to live with horses for several years before they know their nature. I think most vets are afraid of horses. If the horse even blinks at them they hit him with a needle. They want him so sedated he can barely stand, and sometime they put them on the ground.

I had just heard about a young veterinary that had started practicing in Rolling Hills. He was just out of school, but the thing that made me think he might be my man, was he was a real cowboy. He had been a champion bronc rider. I have always wanted to find a vet that knew something about horses. I called a friend that kept his horses up there at the Silver Saddle Club. I knew he would know him. He gave me his name and number, and I called him.

I could hear traffic noise, so I knew he was driving. I asked him, "if he gave a discount for five castrations?"

He thought it over a minute before he asked, "do you actually have five horses that need castrating?"

"As a matter of fact, I do. My name is Graham Peterson, and I have a place in Chatsworth. I have five studs that recently came off the race track. I can't sell them as saddle horses as long as they are studs. I used to do my own, but someone turned me in to animal control and they told me I was breaking the law and couldn't do it anymore."

"When would you like to do this? I want to meet a man that castrates his own horses."

"Your schedule is the deciding factor. You tell me when you can work me in, and that is when I would like to do it."

"How about tomorrow afternoon about two o'clock?"

I gave him the address and said, "I'll be looking for you."

I went in the office and looked at the papers on the five horses. I was surprised by one of them. He had strong bottom breeding. His mother had been by a good Kentucky stud and had been a multi stakes winner. His sire was Indian Hemp, a California stallion that had some success as a sire. He couldn't be compared to the Kentucky sires, but he had done well considering the mares he was getting. The most impressive thing about this horse was he had won six races. Two of them had been in allowance company. There might be some small breeder who needs an inexpensive stallion. If nothing else, he could be used as a teaser. I decided that I would spare him the knife, at least for now.

All five of the horses had decent confirmation, and none of them were beat up too bad. No bowed tendons, or blown out knees. They all looked sound enough to make saddle horses, or maybe even a kid's jumping horse. They were going to make a profit for sure.

All but one of them had won at least one race. Two of them had won two races. That wasn't important, but it impressed the average person on the street. They liked to say their horse won at the race track.

When my exercise rider came over, I told him I needed him at two o'clock. I didn't tell him why. It might scare him away.

The vet pulled in at about two thirty. He put out his hand, and said, "my name is Connie Clarkson by the way."

"My name is Graham Peterson."

"Let's have a look at these horses."

I took him to their stalls and said, "after looking at their breeding, I have decided not to cut the one on the end. He has a really strong bottom line and has won in allowance company. Someone might need a Teaser, or someone might want to breed him to Quarter Horse mares. His wins were all sprinting. I can always cut him if I don't find a customer."

We decided to do it on the grass in the center of the race track. He was good at his job and we had done all four in three hours. When he finished, he told me to keep them in the stall for a week or so and then just light exercise for a couple more weeks. After that they are good to go.

He said, "how long have you been in the horse business?"

"Since I was eighteen."

"How many horses have you owned in that time?"

"I was trying to come up with that figure just a few days ago. I finally decided that I bought and sold approximately five hundred horses a year for thirty years."

"Wow! that's like forty a month. That's a lot of horses."

" It's not as many as it sounds like it is. I have bought twenty head just this week. That is not an unusual week. At the end of next month, I have sixty head of horses coming back from summer camp rental. I will sell them in the week after they come back. I will disperse them through the local auctions. I have a deal with The Border Ranch at Tijuana that I buy eight or ten horses a month. I trade horse with two or three rental stables. A horse that is being ridden by a novice gets sour and starts balking. I trade them a fresh one for a small fee. I furnish all of the Pony boys at the race track horses for their morning ponying. There are twelve of them that I supply, and they average crippling about one a month each. I get calls from guys who want me to buy horses for them at auctions all over the country. I could name a dozen more places I buy and sell horses. I sold a guy who is setting up a breeding farm out by the old Reagan Ranch, fourteen Thoroughbred mares three weeks ago. It all adds up."

He said, "I had no idea that much horse business went on around here. What do they do with all of these horses?"

"On any given Sunday, there may be six different

horse shows taking place, with two hundred entrants at each show. On the same day there may be forty cowboys at each of six roping arenas. There are three or four thousand race horses at the race tracks. Griffith Park has four or five hundred horses for rent and several thousand boarded. There are several hundred breeding farms raising race horses. The Arab breeders probably account for a couple of thousand also and they have their own shows. It goes on and on. I heard that you had just came to this country. Is that true? Have you been over to Griffith Park?"

 "I've only been in this country about six months. I'm from Montana and I haven't been anywhere yet."

"It's too late to go today. The first day you have some time I will show you around a little. Make me a bill and I'll write you a check. He came in the office and I wrote him a check. When I opened my check book a check fell out, and he picked it up. I said that is a check for eight head I sold the Will Rogers Polo club two weeks ago. I had forgot to deposit it."

"I have to worm a horse in the morning at nine o'clock. That's all I have scheduled for the entire day. I would love to see some of the country. Is tomorrow a good time for you?"

"Tomorrow would be fine. Come whenever you are done with your business." I watched him drive out to the street, and I couldn't help thinking that having only one little procedure for the whole day wasn't a good thing. He wasn't getting rich yet.

He showed up about ten thirty. I told him to lock his truck, and we would go in mine. I went on the streets rather than getting on the freeway because I wanted to show him a stable. I told him this was the first place where Ronald Reagan kept his horses. The guy that has it now is a really good friend of mine. I want you to know up front that you should never do any work for him. He just flat out will not pay.

I drove over to the area that we all know as the river bottom. It is the area where most of the stables are. There are a few stables scattered around the park, but this is where most of them are clustered. I explained that the park was donated by a wealthy man with the explicit clause that it was to be used for horses, and horse activities. It is over four thousand acres with bridle trails all through it. I drove down the street first and let him see the huge stables along the front of the park. I pointed out different things. That stables rents horses and they have a hundred and seventy-five in their string. That stable doesn't rent, but they have two hundred borders. I drove back to the indoor polo building. They have indoor polo here once a month on Saturday night. They draw a huge crowd. I don't know if they come to see polo or come to see the movie stars that are always here.

I then took him around to the outside polo grounds. There were five guys out there knocking the ball around. One of them was William Devane and one of them was Alex Cord. I said I would stop and introduce you, but they are both mad at me right now. I put

William on a horse that was way over trained for him to ride and he almost killed himself. He bought the horse but he is mad because all of his friends saw the wreck. Alex is mad at me because I stole one of his exercise riders to gallop horses for me at the race track. Those girls turn into real horse backers. They gallop four at a time. They ride one and pony two on the right and one on the left. They take two or three sets a day, and after a couple of months they are riders. Most of them were pretty good before they started, but they get really good. This was the second time I had stolen one, and he told me if I did it again, he would have me killed.

I took him over to a giant barn across the quad. I told him that it had four-hundred stalls and a long waiting list. While we were sitting there, Zsa-Zsa Gabor and Christine Williams, the Play Boy Star of the Year, came riding out together. I knew Christine because I had sold her a horse a few months ago.

There was a complex called The Pickwick that had a restaurant and a bowling alley. It had an ice-skating rink and a pool room. I took him there for lunch. After we were finished, I told him that several of the movie wranglers hung out in the pool room and we should walk down there. We went back and there were four wranglers in there and four guys that just hang around. I was looking for Wally, because he claimed his brother was a champion bronc rider.

I said, "Wally, what was your brother's name?"

He said, "Henry Clay."

Connie said, "no shit, you are Clays brother?"

"Yeah, do you know my brother?"

"I know him too well. He one pointed me at the Calgary Stampede for a big purse I needed to win."

"You are a rider then?"

"Retired, but tell him the next time you talk to him that Connie Clarkson said hello."

"What are you doing in these parts?"

I spoke up, "lay off Wally, he is my Veterinarian." I knew that Wally was thinking a rider might be here trying to horn in on the movie action. Wally can be kind of aggressive, and I didn't feel like fighting him today.

On our way home I told him that there was a horse auction every Friday night, and if he wanted to go to one, give me a call.

He asked if I was going this Friday night. I told him that I went every Friday, just for the gossip. He said he would like to go. I told him they started selling tack at seven and they usually started on horses about nine. I liked to be there before seven, and it was a two-hour drive. He said he would be at my place by four.

I went in my office and continued to go through my rolodex. Every person who might be a customer for a Thoroughbred mare went on my list. Now I also started a list of people who might need a teaser or a Thoroughbred stallion to breed to Quarter horse mares. I entered the email addresses of the people I put on the list. When I was finished making the list, I had forty on the mare list and twelve on the stallion list. I scanned the papers on the mares first I made a file of the papers and attached it to a short letter telling them these mares were for sale at very reasonable prices. I sent the emails to the list. I then scanned the papers on the stallion and attached it to a short letter explaining all of the things this horse would qualify for. I also added the price of Two thousand dollars. I then sent the emails to everyone on his lists.

I had never tried this broadcast form of sales before. The idea had occurred to me on the drive from Arkansas. I decided to give it a try. If I don't get any reaction, I will call the people on my list. I have done that before and it is very time consuming.

The emails went out about five o'clock. I was thinking this would be about the time they were quitting for the day. I had just finished eating dinner, when I received my first call. It was from my friend with the railroad ties barn. He wanted a total rundown on the horse. I spent a half hour pointing out the good points of the horse as an inexpensive but useful stallion. He offered me fifteen hundred for the horse. He said he was going to resell the horse and that was all he could pay. I told him if he would pay in cash so I didn't have to show it on my books I would do a deal. He agreed and I delivered the horse the next morning. I didn't really want cash because I didn't want it on my books. I wanted cash because more than one person had told me he was bad pay. I was taking no chances on not being paid.

I was a little disappointed when two days passed without a single call about the mares. I was debating whether I should resend the email or just give up and start making calls. A breeder out near Riverside, called me. He told me I had made a mistake with my email. Most people will not call on something for sale if there is not a price on the item. People are shy about being put in a position of having to say no, when the price turns out to be too high. I would suggest you re-send your email with a price on each mare. I thanked him for the advice and went in to my computer and put a price on each mare. It took me a while to put a price on them because I had to look at the breeding and think about how much they were actually worth. The prices ran from five to nine thousand. I inflated each price by one thousand to give them a little room to negotiate. I sent the email again. It went about quitting time again. I would give it a couple of more days. I had intended to go to the Wednesday auction in Chino but because there were no calls about the mares I didn't bother to go. Chino is in the horse farms area and I thought I might get a little action there.

Tomorrow is Friday, and I had hoped for a few calls that would bring them out to look at horses over the weekend. The phone was quiet all day and I was thinking about my next move. Friday morning, I had two calls, and they were both serious buyers. I was feeling better about the email broadcast. By mid-afternoon I had four calls and three appointments for Saturday. I was on the phone with my fifth call when Connie drove up. I made an appointment for Sunday morning. I told them to call before they came because a couple of people were going to look on Saturday. I didn't want them to make the drive, if the horse they were interested in was already sold.

We were on the freeway heading for El Monte when I got another call. I asked which mare they were interested in, and he said all of them. I asked if he knew where my place was and he said no. I gave him my address and told him to come tomorrow at any time. I would be there all day.

Connie was asking about the auction. When I told him that within fifty miles there was an auction every night except Sunday and Monday. From time to time there was one on Sunday. He couldn't believe there were enough horses to supply that many auctions. I told him that I didn't know how to prove or disprove it but I had read several times that there were more horses in Southern California than in the state of Texas.

I drove into the auction complex and was early enough to get a decent parking place. Connie was looking around with awe. He asked why there were so many corrals. I told him that the owner supplied Alpo and Cal Can with horses. They each use a hundred a week. I explained, that he has buyers all over the country. If he doesn't have four or five hundred horses on hand, he gets nervous.

We walked over to the auction barn. In the alley behind the barn there were forty or fifty horses tied waiting to be sold. In the auction ring there were saddles and tack from lead ropes and saddle blankets to bridles.

The cowboys and horse traders were starting to group in gossip bunches out front of the barn. We joined one of the groups and I said this Is Connie Clarkson. He used to ride broncs and now he knocks them down and cuts their nuts off.

From there we did more listening than talking. The only talking I did, was asking questions when they were talking about something or someone that interested me. Gossip was an important part of my business. One of the first things I learned in this business, was you needed to keep up with what other guys are doing. The greatest guy in the world will throw you under the bus when he gets desperate. I have seen guys that are honest as they can be suddenly cheat a good friend because he was overextended and desperate. When I hear that someone has fallen on hard times, I steer clear of him. I may loan him a few bucks, but I won't do business with him. I don't want to put him in a position of having to cheat me.

Connie went in and watched the tack sell for an hour. He came out and said this stuff sells cheap. I told him it was cheap stuff, and most of it was from Mexico.

He went in and took a seat in the grandstand when they started to sell horses. He watched for two hours. He had never been to a horse auction before, and was fascinated.

On the way home he asked a hundred questions. He asked about procedure. He asked about different people. He asked about the horses and where they came from. I tried to answer each of his questions but some of them had complicated answers that had different answers in different situations.

At one point he said, "I have been around horses all my life and thought I was a competent horseman. It blows my mind to realize I don't know zip."

Knowing horses is not the same thing as knowing the horse business. You have to live with horses for a considerable time to know their nature. You have to be in the horse business for a considerable time to understand what makes money and what doesn't. The horse business looks so easy. You buy a horse and sell him for more than you paid. In the last thirty years I have seen maybe two hundred guys come into the business. Most of them didn't last a year.

There are two things that doom you to failure. New people ignore or fail to recognize that the profit or loss is made when you buy the horse, not when you sell the horse. If you pay too much there is no profit to be made. The thing that destroys most of them is they don't factor in upkeep. For example, If I buy a horse for two hundred dollars, and try to sell him for four hundred dollars when he is really worth one hundred, I am kidding myself. It costs me twenty-five dollars a month to keep a horse. I have seen guys keep a horse for a year or more trying to get the profit. He now has five hundred in his one-hundred-dollar horse. If you multiply that by the ten horses he bought when he started, he now has five thousand in horses worth a thousand. He goes on until the weight of the upkeep crushes him.

I started small and made all of my mistakes in small enough amounts that it didn't break me. I discarded all of the things that didn't make money and only kept things that were profitable. I won't ever be a billionaire, but I make a comfortable living and feel like I am on vacation. I love what I do. I am an impulsive man and I am free to follow all of my impulses.

We made the barn about midnight. He thanked me for taking him and went home. He listened to all of my rambling without complaining. I like him.

I didn't have to do any clean up on the mares. Barbara had cleaned them up to go to auction. They were all clipped and trimmed, and looked great. I had made several copies of their papers so the people could have them as we looked at the horses.

The guy that had called about liking all of them came driving in at seven o'clock. I had just got to the barn and wasn't tied on yet. He was a big burly guy that looked like he could play guard for the Rams. He looked fifty but could be older. He was driving an Escalade that needed washing. He didn't ask many questions and I took him out to look at the mares. He turned out to be pretty thorough. He looked each mare over carefully and checked the papers against their markings.

 He turned to me and said, "you have these mares priced at thirty-nine thousand. Would you deliver them to Twentynine Palms for thirty-five thousand?"

"If it is in cash I would."

"I can handle that. Can you do it today?"

"You hand me the money and I start loading horses."

He smiled and said, "I don't blame you for being cautious. I'm a stranger and acting a little weird. My daughter has just graduated from college, and she wants to try breeding horses. She says this is a nice little band of horses with decent breeding. I am going to buy them for her. I am acting so quickly because I have to catch a plane to Nova Scotia in the morning, and won't be back for six months. I am the Forman on a drilling rig up there. I have the money in the car. We can do the deal right now."

He went to the car and I met him in the office. He counted the money on my desk and I gave him the papers. He gave me the address and said he was going to eat breakfast. I called the people that had appointments an apologized for selling the mares before they had a chance to see them. I called the house and had my wife come down to the office. I gave her the money and told her to put it in the bank. It was Saturday and the bank closed at noon.

I hooked up my trailer and drove down to the paddock. I had lead ropes and was just starting to catch the mares when Connie drove in. He saw me at the paddock a drove on back where I was. He said that he had some spare time and was going to check on the horses to make sure there was no infections. He asked what I was doing? I told him I had sold the five mares and was delivering them. He helped me catch them and load them. He asked where I was going, and asked if he could ride along. I was glad for the company. He locked his truck and we got on the road.

When he said he hadn't been anywhere, he meant it. He gawked at everything along the way. The place at Twentynine Palms was nice. She had a twenty-stall barn that had just been built, and several five- or ten-acre paddocks. The hay barn was full and looked like about fifty tons. She was set up for a good start. She was an attractive young lady, maybe twenty pounds overweight. She gave her name as Carolyn Wren and Connie went to her like a homing pigeon. I was trying to put the horses away and they were too busy with their conversation to help me. I couldn't tell which one was the seducer and which one was the seduce. I asked her if she was interested in a few more mares, if I ran across them? She gave me her number and told me she would like to have a total of twelve or fourteen mares. She didn't think she could handle more than that.

As we left, I noticed that he was really paying attention to all of the turns. I strongly suspected that he was coming back as soon as we got home. We talked on the way home but talking was finished when we pulled in the driveway. He was out of my truck before I came to a full stop, and in his truck and gone. There was not a doubt in my mind where he was going.

Earl telling me he didn't know how to dispose of his retired horses, made me think I might be missing a profit source. I have to check in with the pony boys at the race track. Three or four of them owe me money. They never offer to pay. You have to go and ask them for it. In the beginning I had a problem asking for payment, but after five years of it I have no problem at all. I would go to the track in the morning and spend some time collecting and spend some time visiting with trainers.

I took a look at the four cut horses to be sure they were healing clean. There was no reason for infection but I sure didn't want any. They all looked good enough to start a little exercise tomorrow. The races were at Hollywood Park and I was there by seven.

I went by the pony barn and caught two of the guys that owed me money. One of them gave me four hundred, and the other gave me two hundred. I wrote it down in my little tally book. They both still owed me over a thousand each. I was really thinking about stopping my business with them. Now that I wasn't at the track on a regular basis anymore, it was too much trouble trying to collect.

I walked over to the kitchen, and there were not many people there yet. I had bacon and eggs and a Dr Pepper for breakfast. A couple of jockeys were having coffee at a table and three guys were playing cards at a table in the corner. I don't know why they were here so early. I finished my breakfast and went out to walk the barns.

I visited six different trainers that were friends. I just had normal conversations. How are they running? Are you winning any Races? But somewhere in the conversation I inserted a little bit about the owners not being able to get rid of retired horses. I told them to call me if any of their owners had that problem. A couple of them said they had the problem in the past and would remember me in the future.

The track closes at ten o'clock and I went back to the kitchen. In the next hour or two, half of the people at the track will pass through. It is a cafeteria for them to eat. It is a lounge for them to play cards are just sit and visit with friends. I stayed a couple of hours and talked with five or six more trainers. I passed on my story of taking retired horses that they wanted to get rid of. I even found one guy who had one in his barn right now. The horse was done racing and the owner didn't know what to do with him. I gave him my card and told him to call me if the owner wanted him gone. He asked how much I was paying. I laughed, and told him that I would pick him up for free. I told him that was the best deal he was going to find. He said he would let me know and left.

I was sitting at a table talking to another trainer when my phone rang. I answered and the trainer said, "I talked to the owner, and he said pick him up."

"I'll pick him up in the morning when the track closes. Would you pull his papers for me?"

He said he would and I hung up. The trainer I was sitting with, asked, "what was that all about?"

I said, "a trainer had a horse that was finished as a race horse and the owner had no need for him. I agreed to take him off of his hands."

"I have one like that in my barn. Would you pick mine up also?"

"Give me your barn number and pull his papers for me. I'll pick him up in the morning when the track closes."

I brought my trailer but they wouldn't let me in until the track closed of course. I went by trainer A and picked up his horse. He was a gelding so I wouldn't need to castrate him. I went to trainer B and he brought out his horse and it was a mare. I was really surprised. I said you never said yours was a mare. He said you never asked me. I said your right, and loaded her on the trailer. I went back to the ranch and turned them out in a paddock. I went in the office to look at their papers. I hoped that she had a little breeding but I had never heard of either of her parents. I looked at the back of her papers and she had won two races. She had run too cheap and it made her ineligible to race here in Southern California. But she could race in other places. I called a friend that was training at Turf Paradise and asked if he had a stall for another horse. He said he did, and I took the mare on over there.

He called me in a couple of days and said she was pretty fit. He asked where I wanted to run her? I told him to run at the bottom. He said someone may claim her at the bottom. She has won twice in California. I said run her at the bottom, and if she dies, she dies. He called me back four days later, to tell me she had won a non-winner of three race for three thousand claiming. Where did I want to run her now? I said she is out of conditions and will have to run in open company. Run her at the bottom. Two weeks later she won a three thousand claiming and there were three claims on her. He called to give me the bad news. I didn't tell him that she had made seven thousand dollars in a month, and I didn't tell him she was given to me for free.

While this was going on, I was at the ranch grinding out a living. The exercise rider was riding the five geldings every day with a western saddle and teaching them to be a saddle horse. They were doing well enough for me to try to sell them.

I had a call from Barbara in Texas and she asked if I could buy a few more mares. I asked, "what do you have in mind?"

She said, "her father had told her she must sell twenty of her mares. She had loaded the van which he didn't know only held six. That had got him off her back until now. He just realized that she had not sold twenty head. She wanted to know if I could buy some better mares at a better price?"

I told her, "to email me the pedigrees of the mares she wanted to sell, and the price she wanted for each one."

She had done that, but the prices were too high for me. I had looked up every mare and made an estimate of what they were worth to me. Her price for twelve horses averaged almost ten thousand, with several of them being over ten thousand. I could only pay an average of six thousand with three of them being under five thousand.

I called her back and told her that my area wouldn't support the prices she was asking. I told her I would email the list and what I would pay for each horse. I didn't intend to insult her, but that was the prices I felt I could pay and still make a few dollars. She said she understood my position and would talk to me after she got my email. I didn't hear back from her and figured she was shopping my prices. If she was shopping horse by horse, I wouldn't hear from her until tomorrow or the next day.

The next day I had a call from The Border Ranch telling me he had five for me to pick up. I told him I would be there this afternoon. I hooked up my trailer and headed for San Ysidro. The owner wasn't there when I reached the Ranch so I had a chance to look over each horse before I loaded. I didn't see a single candidate for a saddle horse prospect. I drove straight to El Monte and sold them to the owner of the auction. I made a hundred- and twenty-five-dollars profit. After gas, I made a hundred bucks. WOW!

When I came back to the ranch my computer was showing a new email. I opened it and she had sent me a new price list for the mares. I checked them against my list. There were eight of the horses that were at the price I had offered. I took the best six of those and called to tell I could only haul six and I would take those six on the first trip. She agreed, and I told her I would leave tomorrow.

I had just ended the call when Connie came driving in. He came in the office and said, "I see you have been hauling horses."

"I bought five head at San Ysidro and sold them in El Monte. It wasn't a big day but it was profitable. What is up with you?"

He said, "nothing is going on and I am bored to death. You seem to be the only person with any action. I thought I would come and see what's going on with you."

"I am going to Texas in the morning to pick up six mares I bought over the phone. You want to ride along?"

"I sure wish I could. Just about the time we hit the Texas border I would get a call for some emergency. I envy you. You march to your own drum, and do or don't do, according to how you feel about it."

"It may appear that way, but that is not always the truth."

He hung around a couple of hours and wished me luck on the trip and went home. I had been dying to ask him about Carolyn, but I don't know him that well yet. Some can take kidding and some can't. I didn't want to test him yet.

I left early in the morning. I wanted to be clear of the city before the go to work rush hour. The rush hour here lasted about three hours. It is brutal. I went toward the border because I was going to take the ten. I had an uneventful trip and was there in twenty-four hours.

My GPS took me right to the ranch. It was a nice place and had about two hundred acres under irrigation for her horses. She was there waiting and we transacted our business. I paid her in cash and asked for a receipt in case a brand inspector stopped me. I have had it happen crossing some of these western states. Arizona is really bad about doing that.

We talked for a little while. She said that my appraisals were closer to the true value than hers. No one is willing to meet my prices. I am hoping that selling this bunch will stall my dad off again. If not, I may be calling you again. I told her that I was just a phone call away. Feel free to call me anytime you need my help. For that matter you can call me even if you don't need my help.

I loaded the horses and headed for home. It would take longer going back because I had to stop and feed and water the horses every three hours. I felt good and was thinking I could drive for eight or ten hours before my first nap. I Had a good bunch of mares and I was sure they were going to be profitable.

I put a thumb drive in the player and listened to the blues played by some of the greatest guitarist in the world. Some old and some new but all great. Blues is as American as you can get and I love it.

The miles rolled by and time went by smoothly. It was a good trip but I was glad to eventually see the ranch. It was going to be dark in an hour. I turned the mares out in one of the paddocks and went to the house and went to bed.

I didn't wake up until eight o'clock in the morning. I got up and had breakfast. I checked the messages on my phone and returned a couple of calls. That were personal rather than business.

I went back to the barn and everything looked good. I checked on the mares in the paddock and was happy they all were at peace in the grass. I went in the office and scanned the papers into my computer. I called Carolyn and told her I was sending her the information on some mares I had for sale. I put the price with each horse and emailed them to her.

My rider had come to work and was riding one of the horses around on the ranch. He was using him as a normal ranch horse. He stopped him, and stood for a while. He backed him up, and he put him in a rocking horse cantor. I asked him if all of them were going that well? He said they were all ready to sell.

The only thing I had invested was the buck and a quarter to have them cut and a few days of feed.

I called a lady that had an English riding academy I told her I had five Registered Thoroughbred geldings for sale, and if she took all of them, I would take five hundred a horse. She asked how old they were? I told her I had three six-year-olds, one five-year old, and one seven. She asked if I was going to be around all afternoon. I told he I was, and she said as soon as one of her riders showed up, she would come over. I told my rider to hang around, I might need him.

I brought all of the horses in and put them back in the box stalls. I didn't want them to be hard to catch, and I wanted that paddock for them to ride the horses in. It was two hours before they showed up. She had brought a girl that looked about thirteen. She got out of the car with her saddle on her arm.

I said to Joan, let's look at them first. There is no need to saddle and ride one you don't like. We started with the first stall. I took him out of the stall and walked him out in front of the barn in the sunshine. She walked around him checking him all over. She said this one will do. I put him back in the stall and brought the next one. We went through all five of the horses without her rejecting one horse.

We went back to the first stall and I held him while the teeny bopper saddled him. I legged her up and pointed her at the paddock gate. She walked him to the gate and Joan asked her to trot him around a couple of times. She did, and on the second lap Joan asked her to canter him he cantered nice and easy twice around and Joan said take him back to the barn.

We went through the same routine on each horse, and not one of them made a bobble. I was proud of my rider. She asked what I had to have for all five of them. I said come on Joan. You are going to sell these horses for two thousand each. And you think I should take less than five hundred. If you are broke, I'll loan you a hundred, but don't try to scam me. She asked if I was going to deliver them. I told her I would. I noticed my kid flirting with her kid. I hooked up my trailer and he helped me load them. I told him he could ride over with me and see where she rode every day. He jumped right in the truck. I went in the office and got their papers.

We drove over to Joan's stable and my kid and her kid

put the horses away as I unloaded them. Joan went in the house, and came back with twenty-five hundred dollars and I gave her the papers. On the way home my rider said her rider was really cute. I said I didn't notice but I'll take your word for it. Isn't she a little young? He said I thought so at first. It turns out she will be eighteen next month, she looks young because she is so small.

I hadn't heard back from Carolyn, and I figured they were too expensive for her. It was Friday and I went in to clean up and get ready to go to the auction. I was a little late getting there and had to park way out in the boondocks. I could hear them selling tack already, as I walked to the barn. There were four of my friends standing outside the barn talking. I stopped to say hello and one of them said you friend is in watching the tack sale. I assumed he was talking about Connie, and I went in to say hello. He was sitting in the grandstand and sitting next to him was Carolyn. She saw me walk in and held up her hand in a sort of a wave. I walked over and said are you folks having fun? Connie said, Carolyn has never been to a horse auction. I thought she might like to see one. I said, I think she will find it interesting. I have to go listen to the gossip. I'll talk to you later.

I went out front to talk with the guys standing around. One of them told me that Joe Bates had died of lung cancer. I knew it was coming soon, but it was still a sad occurrence. I did hear something of interest. One of the guys said he had sold two horses to a mutual friend of ours and the check had bounced. Information of that sort was important in our business. It might save me money later on.

After we had all talked about the last week. I went out back to look at the horses that were going to sell tonight. Connie and Carolyn were doing the same thing. I took a walk by the line of tied horses and didn't see anything of interest. I told them I had seen most all of these before, and I was going home. Carolyn said she would call me in the morning about the mares. She evidently has some interest.

On the way home I was thinking of Joe and his daughter. I was worried about her. I didn't know if she was capable of taking care of herself. I would go by tomorrow and talk to her.

When I had not heard from Carolyn by ten o'clock, I drove over to check on Joe's daughter. She was sitting on a log in the shade. The place was bare. No horses, and no one around. I asked her where were the horses, and she told me Sam had come and bought everything. He bought the horses and tack and everything. I asked what she was going to do now. She said she didn't know what to do. She said she couldn't do anything until he paid her. I said, "wait a minute. Are you telling me that Sam bought your horses and all of your tack and didn't pay you?"

She started to cry, and said, "I didn't know what to do. He told me he would give me twenty-five thousand dollars for everything."

"Why are you just sitting here?"

"I don't know where to go, I don't have any money."

I said, "who owns this property?"

"A guy named Jim. He comes on the first day of the month for his rent."

"How much is the rent?"

"I think it's three hundred dollars."

"Is the house ok for you to live in?"

"It's fine but I don't have any money for the rent."

I said, "first thing is to get you some food. Come with me and we'll go to the grocery store."

She got in my pickup and on the way to the store I asked her if she had eaten today yet? And she said she ran out of food yesterday. I pulled into Burger King and took her in for a hamburger and fries. I had a Dr Pepper and she asked for coffee. After we ate, I took her to Walmart, and we filled a basket to the top.

I asked her how she got around and she said she had a bicycle but is was broke. I took her over to the bike department and we picked out a girl's bicycle with a big basket. I put everything in the truck and took her home. I told her I would be here on the first to pay her rent and gave her fifty dollars in case she needed anything.

I drove over to Sam's place and the more I thought about it the madder I became. I walked into his office and there were three or four horsemen sitting there talking. I said. "you might be the biggest asshole in the country."

He said, "what's your problem?"

"You wait for a guy to die, and then you go up there and take everything his mentally challenged daughter has. You told her you were going to give her twenty-five thousand dollars. You hauled everything she had away and didn't even leave her something to eat. She has been sitting with no money and no food waiting for you to bring her twenty-five thousand dollars You may be the rottenest prick I ever met."

"You don't know what you are talking about. This is not something you should be accusing me of in front of people."

"I know exactly what I'm talking about. I just bought her some groceries. If you think these are the only people that will hear about you. You don't know me. I intend to spend the next month driving all over the country telling every person in the horse business what a cheap thieving no good prick you are."

"I told her I would pay her by the first of the month."

"No, you didn't. You told her you would send a check with the guys who were coming to pick up her horses. Anyway, the first of the month is two days away, where is the money?"

"This is none of your business. This is between me and

her."

"You are full of shit. I have a letter from Joe asking me to take care of her. That makes me her guardian. Where is the dam check?"

"I'll write you a check but I am going to postdate it until the first."

"No, you're not. If you postdate it, it is not a check. It's a promissory note. I will hold it until the first but you are not going to postdate it."

"You are not going to tell me how to handle my business."

"No, but I will tell everyone in the world how you handle it. If you don't give me a check for her right now, I will make sure no one will ever accept a check or the promise of one from you."

"I should get up and whip your ass."
"I think you are about twenty years past getting that done, but I would love for you to try. Jump up and take your best shot. If you don't write me a check right now for her, I will tell everyone that these friends of yours witnessed you refusing to pay her. What's it going to be big shot?"

He jerked his check book out of his desk and wrote her a check. He handed it to me and I looked at it carefully. I didn't intend to let him get away making some mistake that voided the check. "If you try to say later that you didn't sign this, I have three people here who saw you sign a twenty-five-thousand-dollar check to pay for horses and tack to Jean Bates."

As I walked to the door, he said, "don't ever come on my property again."

I said, "don't worry about that. I don't deal with thieves." I left the door standing wide open, and walked away forever from his door.

I didn't feel very strong about the chance of getting the money. I had at least a little leverage. If that check didn't cash, I could bring him up on bad check charges and because it was for a sizeable amount, and for goods that were taken it was a fraud. I think I would have a good chance of putting him in jail.

It was midafternoon and I had still not heard from Carolyn. I decided that she wasn't a buyer and I would send another email to all of the people I had sent to before. I had generated interest before.

I had thirty-nine thousand in the six mares. According to my appraisal they were worth fifty thousand. That wasn't enough profit for that much investment and the hauling involved. I wasn't going to lower the price. It was a well-bred bunch of mares.

I had just turned off the television, and was headed for the bedroom when my phone rang. I answered and it was Carolyn. She apologized for calling so late. She said she was ten thousand dollars short and had gone to her dad's brother to borrow the money. They had turned it into a family gathering, and she had just got home. She said if I could deliver them some time tomorrow, she was ready for them. I told her it would be after lunch and she said that would be great.

When I finished breakfast, I drove over to talk to Jean. She was sitting in the shade, rubbing on her bicycle. I asked, "who rented the horses when Joe was here?"

She said, "she rented them, but Joe helped her when she was busy."

"If I had someone to help you, do you think you could do it without Joe."

She said, "I think so. I have done it a long time."

"You know how to sign them up and take the money? Do you have any trouble making change?"

"I make change ok. The only trouble I have is people that ask for a certain horse when he is out already. I don't know what to do then."

"I want to make you a deal. I'll put horses and saddles here and we will be partners. We will split the profit fifty/fifty. How does that sound?"

"That sounds great. I love the horses."

"I have horses at a summer camp and I will be picking them up in a week. I will bring some of them here. How many horses did you have before?"

"We had eighteen most of the time."

"Did you need more or was that enough?"

"Most of the time it was enough."

I went back to the farm and talked to my rider. I told him that I needed him to work at a small rental stable. He needed to be there on Saturday and Sunday for the rental business. The things that needed to be repaired or changed around he could do during the week. He could take his days off on Monday and Tuesday. I explained that Jean was not quite normal and I expected him to get along with her. She is a nice person and if I find out you are mistreating her, I will tear your head off.

I hooked up my trailer and he helped me load the horses. I went to Twentynine Palms, and Carolyn was pleased with the mares. There is always a little anxiety when you buy horses sight unseen. She said she had spent all her money to buy this load and she wouldn't be buying anymore for a while. I told her to call me when she got flush again. She laughed, and said she would do that.

It was getting late when I got home. I watched television for a while and went to bed. In the morning I went to Jean's place to wait for Jim to come for his rent. While I waited, I walked around looking at the place. It looked kind of shabby and needed some repair. I had brought a little pad and I made some notes of what needed to be done. The place was not large, and the only thing going for it, was a lot of undeveloped property around it for people to ride on.

Jim showed about eleven. He was older than I expected. He was seventy or eighty and looked unhealthy. I introduced myself and told him about Joe dying and that I was taking care of Jean and would be paying her rent. He didn't seem to care as long as he got his rent. We talked for a little bit, and I asked him how large the property was. He said it was a little under five acres. I also asked him if he had plans to sell it. I told him it needed some repair and I didn't want to spend a lot of money if he was thinking of selling it. He said he wouldn't sell it unless someone offered him a lot of money for it. I asked what was a lot of money and he said a hundred thousand dollars. I said that is a lot of money.

I went over to the barn and picked up my kid. I really can't call him kid any longer. He graduated high school this year. He is eighteen now and wants to be in the horse business. I took him back to Jeans and introduced him to Jean. I said Jean this is Billy Knudson and he is going to be your helper. She shook his hand very formal and said, it's nice to meet you.

I had put my tool box in the back of the truck, and I grabbed a tape measure. The first thing I checked was the horse corral. I couldn't have horses running all over the neighborhood. It had four broken post and it need an extra post where the span was too long. I needed a top rail of two by six around the entire corral. The post were set eight feet apart and there were thirty-two of them. I needed a metal gate. The one that was there was about to fall apart. I needed a lot of four-inch nails. I took Billy with me to get the lumber.

This was going to be an expensive undertaking. Just this first little dab was five hundred dollars. I left Billy off with the lumber and I went to Tractor Supply for a metal gate. I didn't buy a post hole digger because I had seen one in the tack room. I had asked Jean if anything on her little house needed repairing and she told me no.

By the time I was back with the gate, he had replaced two of the posts. He was going to be all right. I walked out behind the corral to see if there was room to put in a larger corral. There was room but I didn't want to buy lumber for a big corral. In the past I had built corrals from used telephone poles I would go to the power company yard and see if they had any on hand. The other thing bothering me was there was no place to store hay. Jean was cleaning the tack room and I went over and asked her were they kept their hay. She showed me a dozen wood pallets stacked by a tree. She said they stacked the hay on the pallets to keep them off the ground and they had a tarp they put over it, but Sam's guys took the tarp.

I was helping dig a post hole to give Billy a break. My phone rang and it was one of the summer camps. He told me I could pick up the horses any time he was finished with them. I told him I would be there in the morning. He had eighteen, so that would be a three-trip haul.

I helped Billy finish setting the posts. We started nailing the top rail and got about half finished before it started getting dark. I took Billy back to the ranch and his trailer. We had put his bike in the back of the truck. He had worked hard all day and shouldn't have to ride his bike home. I told him to go right to the stable tomorrow and I would be there to help him as soon as I could.

I went to the camp early and started loading my tack. I had one saddle missing. The owner wasn't around yet so I didn't know if it was around somewhere or not. I had brought a box of cheap nylon shipping halters. I started loading horses. I had my trailer full and he still had not arrived. I went on home with the first load. I turned them out in the big paddock and the went right to grazing. The stall cleaners had unloaded the tack while I unloaded the horses. I had them set the saddles and equipment in the shed row of the barn. I went back for the second load.

When I drove in the camp, I saw the owner loading stuff from his office into his car. He came down to see me while I was haltering and loading the horses. Before I could ask him about it, he said one saddle had disappeared. The deal we made was each saddle was worth a hundred dollars. He gave me a hundred dollars and said he didn't know what happened to it. It just disappeared. I finished loading the second bunch of horses and took them to the ranch. I could buy this caliber of saddle any Friday night for seventy-five dollars. So that didn't bother me. I turned this load out in the paddock and went back for the last load.

I was in a ghost town at the camp. No one around and the buildings all closed up. He hadn't said anything to me about locking the gate. I didn't know what to do. He might not be back until next year, and he may have just gone to get something to eat and was coming right back. I loaded my horses and when I pulled through the gate I went back and closed it. I put the lock in the chain but I didn't lock it. I dropped this load off and went over to the stables.

Billy had Jean holding one end of the board up for him while he nailed the other end. It was working ok and they were nearly finished. They nailed the last two rails up while I brought the gate over and started looking at how I wanted to mount it. When they finished Billy came over and he and I mounted the gate. It opened and closed nicely, and I needed to pick up a piece of chain to lock it at night when it wasn't in use.

We needed something to water the horses with. They had been using rusty old wash tubs. They had three of them and none of them looked like they would hold water. The water troughs at Tractor Supply were very expensive. Billy said the Habitat store always had a lot of bathtubs out back. We should go check them out. I thought that was a good idea and that's where we went'. They had a dozen, and we picked out three of them that didn't look as if a horse could injure himself on. The twenty-dollars apiece was worth the money for our use.

I had to go for a load of hay, and I needed a tarp to

cover it with. I also need a long hose to reach the water tubs. I went to Home Depot for a hundred-foot hose and a tarp. I bought a tarp twenty by forty. I was sure that was big enough.

I took Billy over and left him at the ranch I told him to look through the horses in the paddock for nice horses. I told him there were a lot more coming in the next few days so only pick what looked good. If he found any he liked, he was to put them in the other paddock and make sure they had water. I told him I wouldn't be back for four hours and to take his time. I also told him to pick out the best saddles from the ones in the shed row of the barn. A lot more of them coming also so be picky. I hooked on to my flatbed trailer and went for hay.

When I got back, he had picked four horses that he liked and six saddles. We went to the stables and I un-hooked the trailer and we put the tarp over the hay. Billy had just ridden away on his bicycle when my phone rang. It was another summer camp owner to tell me I could pick up the horses. He only had twelve, but he was the farthest away. It would take as long for his two loads as it had taken for the three trips. I told him I would pick them up in the morning.

I was on the road by seven in the morning and drove in his place at nine. I loaded the saddles and tack first. I loaded the first bunch and was on the road back by nine-forty-five. It was two o'clock before I was fin-ished. I had had two more calls from camp owners, and I was going to be hauling horses for the next two or three days. I picked up Billy and took him to the ranch. I had turned these last horses out in the infield of the race track. I told him to pick out the horses he wanted and put them in the smaller paddock. The ones he didn't want he was to put with the other ones he didn't want. There was another pile of saddles to look through.

When I got back with the first load from this camp, he had only liked two of the horses from the other camp but he had picked six saddles. This camp had eighteen and I only had time for one more load before dark. I got back with the second load and Billy had liked two from the first load and picked four saddles. I turned the horses in the infield and took him back to the stables for his bicycle. I was just sitting down to super when my phone beeped a text. It was the last camp owner telling me I could pick up the horses. I texted back, tomorrow. I was on the road by seven again and did three loads before sundown. Billy had told me he would ride his bicycle to the ranch and sort the horses in the infield.

When it was all over, he had picked twenty horses and twenty-five saddles. I opened one of my tack trunks from the race track to see how many hay nets I had. I had about twenty. I had ten in my trailer that I used on long hauls but I wanted to leave them there. I went to Home Depot and bought twenty, two by fours. I nailed a two by four to the outside of every post sticking six feet in the air. I put an eye bolt at the top of each stud to hang hay nets on. I wouldn't know if it was going to work until I tried it.

From the don't like paddock I loaded six horses and took them to the Chino Wednesday night auction. I didn't stay for the sale and they could mail me a check. I waited to see what they were going to bring before I decided what to do with the others. After commission, they averaged a hundred and a quarter each. I called the owner of the El Monte auction and asked what he would pay for thirty head coming back from summer camp. He said he would pay one thirty. I told him I would start hauling in the morning. I started at seven in the morning and unloaded my final load at five o'clock. I went home and collapsed.

I loaded a few of the saddles and bridles and took them over to the stables, with six horses. It was Saturday and I wanted to have some horses there in case any kids came to ride. I had talked to Billy and he said he would be there by eight. I left the first load of horses and tack, and went back for a second load. I didn't expect any riders since it had been closed for three weeks. But I could hope. When I came with the second load Billy was there and they had hung hay nets and filled the water tubs. Jean had saddled three horses and had them tied out front where anyone going by would see them. I said good for you Jean, you know what to do.

I was in the building they had used as a tack room. It was showing signs of a leaky roof, but the building wasn't too bad. It was useable. I came out to take a look at the roof and Jean was adjusting the stirrups for two little girls about twelve or thirteen. She immediately saddled two more horses and tied them out front. It wasn't a great day but she rented fourteen horses over the course of the day. I had never asked her how much they charged. It was five dollars for the first hour and three every hour after that. She had one pair go for two hours, and she had taken in seventy-six dollars. She was all smiles. I was happy for her.

I had found an old ladder in the back. It scared me to death but I needed to look at the roof. It was old felt paper roofing. It was a miracle it shed water at all. I measured the side from apex to the bottom edge. It was twelve feet, and I hoped that corrugated metal came in twelve feet lengths. The building was twenty feet long. I went to Home Depot and bought twenty-two sheets of metal and a box of screws with a rubber collar on them. The metal sheets were four feet longer than the bed of my pick up. I tied them in well and hung red flags all over them. I made it back to the stable without seeing a police car. I wasn't sure I had a legal Load. I ran over to the ranch and picked up my eight foot step ladder and my screw gun and a power saw.

I put Billy on the top and I stood on the ladder at the bottom. I handed up the sheets and screwed them at the bottom. We had the roof covered in four hours, and I realized I had forgotten a ridge cap and I had to go back again to pick one up. While I was there, I picked up a bunch of saw horse brackets and a stack of two by fours. I needed to make something to set the saddles on.

While Billy screwed the ridge cap on, I made ten eight-foot saw horses. Two saddles to a saw horse and we were in good shape. They near filled the building up. I put one of the wood pallets in the corner to stack saddle pads on. I drove nails all around the wall for bridles. By quitting time, the tack room looked like a tack room instead of a hut.

Sunday was better than Saturday had been. Jean rented twenty-four horses and was absolutely beaming. There is a lot of things Jean doesn't know anything about. She does know how to saddle and rent horses. That is what she has done her whole life and she has it ingrained in her brain. I hoped this worked out so I could keep her doing something that made her feel useful and successful.

Monday morning, I went to the power line yard. I asked the first guy I came to if they had any used power poles, they wanted to get rid of? He said they had a hundred of them, and pointed out the guy in the blue hard hat as the man to talk to. I went to talk to him, and he asked what I was going to use the poles for. I told him I wanted to make a fence around a riding arena. He said for horses? I said yes. I wanted to run a fence around about a half-acre. He said I can't give you these if you are going to stand them up. You have to guarantee me they will only be used for a fence. I have a little horse place and I am trying to put up a fence that will keep horses in without breaking the bank. He asked what kind of trailer I had? I told him I had a twenty-four -foot flat bed. He said I probably could haul two at a time. This is going be a long-time project.

I went down and bought a good chain saw and some heavy-duty nylon strap rachets. I have some that I use for my hay hauling but I like to keep them for hay. He had told me that their poles were thirty feet long, so I would have an overhang. I bought red flags like the house movers use. I went over to the yard and they loaded two poles for me. I strapped them down and put the flags on. He asked how I was going to unload them? I told him I was going to tie them to a tree and drive out from under them. He laughed and said that is one way, I guess. I made three trips on the first day.

In my back and forth trips through the neighborhood, I had come to the conclusion that this whole area was going to be homes within ten or fifteen years. He was pretty close to the mark asking a hundred thousand.

I made three trips a day for five days. I had enough poles to make a pole barn. But he had made me promise not to stand any of them up. Now would come the hard work. I spent a lot of time laying out the corral. There were going to be several trees enclosed in the corral. I didn't see a problem with that. It would give the horses some shade in the summer. I had started thinking of enclosing a quarter acre. By the time I was finished laying it out I had about an acre inside the future fence. I had a huge ball of construction string. I strung it down one side and we marked the post with a stake. I asked Billy if he knew anyone, we could hire to dig holes? He came back the next morning with two guys.

I cut the posts in seven-foot lengths. I wanted three feet in the ground and four foot high. I cut a vee in the top of the post for the pole to lay in. We set the poles in the ground but we didn't fill in around them yet. We struggled a pole over and set it up one end at a time on the vees. The top of the fence measured four foot six. That was perfect, and I put a six-foot level on it. It was one tick off of perfect We jacked the low end up a tad and tamped the dirt around it with a little water added. It was showing perfect and we tamped the other end. I had bought a roll of small chain and a large box of two-inch staples. I cut the chain with my bolt cutters. I had it come down on each side about a foot and a half. I stapled it down with the big staples. We had just built thirty feet of fence. There was some brush that had to be cleared where the fence was going. I had two digging three feet deep holes and one clearing brush. We had three poles up by quitting time. We had the holes dug for first thing in the morning.

We strung six poles down the first side, and made a ninety-degree turn. We had two more poles set by quitting time. The guys had become much faster now that they knew what we were doing. When we finished the far end wall I had us come back and run this end. It would be impossible to get in here with the outside wall up. We had to do some engineering to decide how we were going to put a gate in here. I decided to cut the fence out of the center of the pole rather than an end, which would screw up our distance. It took longer because we had to dig two extra holes. We measured the width of the gate and cut that out of the middle of the pole. When we finished this end of the fence, we ran our string from this corner to the other end corner, and that was our fence. We had a corral one hundred and eighty feet square. Not quite an acre but close. We finished this side of the fence in one day, and it came out perfect at the corner. I was stunned about that. It looked great and I was really pleased. All I had to do now was hang the gate and cut through the back of the little corral.

I paid off Billy's friends. We had not talked about a price, but they seemed to be happy with three hundred each.

The rentals during the week were not very lucrative. Jean had only rented eight horses all week, but she saddled a couple of horses every morning and put them out front. Tomorrow was the first. Jim would be here and I really didn't want him to see what we were doing. I was there early in the morning waiting. He showed up about noon again. I walked out before he could get out of his car, and said I was just about to go get a bite to eat. I would buy lunch if you haven't eaten yet. He said I haven't had lunch. I said you go wherever you would like to eat and I will follow you. He pulled into Culver's.

We went in and ordered burgers and fries and sodas. We went back and found a booth and waited for our food. I gave him an envelope with his rent money in it. I said, "let me ask you a question. If I was to pay you in hundred-dollar bills and tell the title company that I had only paid you a thousand, so the IRS had no idea how much you got. Could you get along on sixty thousand dollars?"

"I think it's worth more than that."

"I'm talking about cash that no one knows you have. No taxes, no nothing. We can close escrow in a week and it's done." Just at that minute the lady brought our food. We sat there eating and I watched him to see if he gave me any clues about what he was thinking. We had finished our meal and were sitting in silence.

To break the silence I said, "have you had any other offers for the property?"

He said, "no, I haven't, but I still think it is worth more than sixty."

"Realistically, how much more do you think it is worth."

"I would have to have at least seventy-five thousand."

"Sixty-five is all I have, but if I borrowed five thousand and made it seventy would you do a deal?"

He was drinking coffee and I was drinking Dr Pepper.

I told him I was going to refill my soda did he want another coffee. He said no and I went to fill my cup. When I came back, he was gazing off into space. I sat down and nursed on my drink and let him think. After a while he said, "let me ask you a question. Why do you want that property?"

I said, "it is a very peculiar reason. Joe Bates just died. He was a long-time friend of mine. He asked me to look after his daughter, who as you know is mentally challenged. The problem is that she as lived there so long that she gets anxiety attacks when she is away from there. The place is run down to the point of not being livable. I had a contractor friend of mine come over and look at it. He told me it would take fifty thousand dollars just to bring it up to code. I can't invest that kind of money in a place that someone could tell me tomorrow I have to get out."

"You just told me that you were going to spend all of your money just buying the property."

"That is correct, but I have an income that will enable me to borrow money. I won't have to spend the entire fifty thousand tomorrow. It will happen over a period of time."

He sat there a long time looking out the window. He finally said, "I am going to sell it to you for seventy thousand. What do we do now?"

"We go down to the title company. They search the records to make sure you own the property. If there is no trouble in the title we come back to their office. I pay you and they transfer the title to me."

I drove him to a title company and opened an escrow with my thousand. I told the girl that there was no financing involved and we would like to close as soon as humanly possible. I told her I was paying all cost. She told me it should close in a couple of days. I said thank you. And I took him back to his car. If he doesn't change his mind in the next couple of days I am in business.

I went home and started collecting money. I had money hid all over the place. I had forty-thousand at home in a floor safe. I had twenty thousand in a safe I had welded to my truck frame. I had fifty thousand in a safety deposit box at the bank. I wasn't going to need that but it was there if I did need it. In the garage at the ranch was a huge walk in refrigerator. It was not turned on and I don't know if it even works. It has a hell of a locking handle on it. I have twenty thousand hidden in the refrigeration apparatus. That puts me over the top.

I fooled around for two days before the call came from the title company. She said that she had talked to Jim and we were meeting at three o'clock for the closing. I put sixty-nine thousand dollars in a canvass bag. I was at the title company half an hour early. I talked to the girl who was doing the closing. I told her that It was worth a thousand to me to have her give Jim sixty-nine thousand dollars in cash with no record of it anywhere. She thought about it for a minute and said I can handle that. Jim came in and we all went into a private office. She explained to Jim that she had sixty-nine thousand in the bag with no record of it. He signed, and she gave him a check for one thousand and the bag. He asked if he could go in another room to count the money. She told him the room next door was vacant. He left and I paid her the fees from the title company and gave her a thousand as a tip. It took Jim almost an hour to count the money. He stuck his head in the door and said we are all square. I went back to the stables.

Billy had done a great job hanging the gate and cutting the fence of the small corral. It looked very professional. I had gone for two more loads of poles while we were building the fence. But now I went back for three more loads. I went in the back where it couldn't be seen and laid out a hay barn. We staked the corners and dug the holes for the corner posts. I knew we would never be able to raise one of the poles to the top for roof beams. We would have to make it from two by tens. I laid it out to be twenty by twenty square I made the edges from two by tens. I made the front higher than the back by four inches. I made the rafters from side to side out of two by eights. We put corrugated metal running from front to back and screwed it down with a vengeance. I didn't want it blowing off. I would wait till we had rain to decide if I needed sides on it.

I hooked on to the trailer and pulled over to the barn.

I backed up to it and Billy and I unloaded the hay that was on the trailer and I took the trailer on back to the ranch.

I had never been in the house and I asked Jean if I could see it. I was floored. I don't know how anyone could live like that. There was an old sofa, a little wood table with two straight back chairs and two twin beds with a sagging mattress. The kitchen had an electric hot plate and a two-foot-high refrigerator. In the bedroom there was a rope nailed from one wall to another, in one corner. It had three or four pieces of clothing on hangers on it. There was a toilet and a sink in the bath room. There was no tub or shower. I went back in the kitchen to make sure there was a sink. There was, but it was very small. I went looking for the power box. I found it on the outside of the house and it was only eighty amps. I didn't know they made one less than a hundred. There was no Television and not even a radio. I gave it a lot of thought, and decided the house was not fixable.

I called two friends of mine. They both dabbled in horses and I knew them very well. One was an electrician and the other was a plumber. The first one to come by was the electrician. I told him I needed a two-hundred-amp box, and I didn't want to get a permit. I told him I would put a pole anywhere he wanted it. I wanted to put a travel trailer in here and I needed the power. I had picked a spot behind the house where I was going to put the trailer. He told me to put the pole behind the house, up close so the wires looked like they still ran to the house. He said the pole should be a foot higher than the house. He shocked me when he told me it would cost two thousand. I had to have it, so there was nothing I could do about the price.

Billy and I dug the hole five feet deep. That was as deep as we could get it. I cut fifteen feet off the pole. We had a hell of a time standing the pole up. If I hadn't cut it off, we would never have stood it up. It looked about a foot taller than the house we put the level against it while we tamped it. I didn't need to have a leaning pole.

The plumber came by and I explained it to him. I needed a travel trailer hooked to the sewer but I didn't want to get a permit. He walked around the house a couple of times and out to the street three or four times. He asked who is going to dig the trench? You show me where you want it and I'll get it drug. He asked where I wanted the sewer to surface. I drove a stake right there. He tied a string to it and walked beside the house and drove a stake. He went with his string and three more stakes right to the street. He said if we hit a pipe or when we got close to the last stake by the street. To stop until he could get out here and take a look.

The electrician came by the next day and put in the power. It was a big job, and he spent the entire day putting it in. Plus, the box and breakers and wire. I didn't realize what the job would entail. His price didn't seem high to me anymore.

I bought two good shovels and a pick in case the ground was hard and brought my two Mexicans over from the ranch. I showed them what I needed done. The plumber had said it needed to be two and a half feet deep. Billy was there to watch over the job. I went shopping for a trailer.

If it had a decent size bump out it could be as small as twenty-six feet. If it didn't have a slide it would have to be at least thirty feet. My wife had made a list of trailers for sale on Craigslist. Two or three of them sounded interesting. One of them was close and I called and went by to see it. It was a twelve-year-old Holiday Rambler. It didn't have a slide but it was thirty feet long. It had a nice kitchen and a really nice bath room. It had a big shower. And a lot of storage for a trailer. The drawback, was that it had two twin beds across from each other. I'm sure that made it hard to sell. I wouldn't have bought it for myself, but it wouldn't bother Jean. She was asking five thousand for it and I could tell she was discouraged about trying to sell it. It didn't look as if it had been used much in its twelve years. Just making conversation I said my wife wouldn't like the sleeping arraignments much. I said, "if I counted out thirty, hundred-dollar bills right now, would you sell me this trailer?"

She said, I'll have to go and call my husband. She came back in about twenty minutes and said he said he would sell it to you for thirty-five hundred. I said

I think I'll buy it. If my wife divorces me over it, it'll be your fault. I counted out the money and she signed the title. I hooked up to the trailer and tested the lights. They all worked and I left. I was bringing it home even if the lights didn't work.

When I reached the stable, I had to decide exactly where I wanted to park it. I had to remove some brush and trash. I backed it in and got really lucky. I hit it right on the nose first try. I didn't have to make any adjustments at all. I plugged in the power and went in and turned on all the lights. Everything looked great. I went over and knocked on Jean's door. I said, "come and see your new home."

She looked at me like I had lost my mind. I motioned for her to come on and she followed me out to the trailer. I had put the steps down and we went in. She was looking around like Alice in wonderland. She was afraid to touch anything.

"It's for you. You're going to live here, go look around." She was scared to death. I didn't know how to make her understand that she was going to live here. I said, "when he gets the sewer hooked up you can move in. It will only be a day or two."

When I went home, I told my wife she had to come over and spend some time showing her how things worked. When you see how she has been living you'll cry.

I took Sam's check to the bank. I told the teller that

I didn't want to cash it yet, I just wanted to know if it was any good. She told me it was good by twenty dollars. I asked her if it was possible to put a hold on the money. She said she could hold it for twenty-four hours. Great. I went home and had my wife take Jean to the bank to open an account with the check. I gave her five hundred, and I told her to take her to Goodwill and buy her some cloths and dishes and pots and pans. I told her that Jean has nothing and needs everything. They went off together, and I hoped it would be a good experience for Jean.

I had called the plumber last night to tell him the trench was finished. He said he would start on it this morning. He came with two guys and they started at the street. They were up to the house in an hour, this wasn't going to take very long. Sid asked me if the trailer was going to be permanent. When I said yes, he suggested I take out the tanks and hook the sewer line directly to the trailer. I needed a regular house toilet to do that. I told him I wanted an elongated toilet. I didn't want one of those little round jobs. He said that was going to extend the entire job to about two thousand. I said I can just afford it, have at it. I thought that would extend the job by a couple of days. These guys knew what they were doing. They were finished before quitting time. They had even run the water pipe out so I had a water faucet beside the trailer to hook the water to the trailer. I went in and flushed the toilet, and it worked like the one in my house. The best part was no more tanks to be dumped. It was great.

Billy rented three horses while this was going on. He did it with no problem, and he was going to be good at this job. He liked people.

The plumbers were leaving and the girls were arriving. The girls came back with the whole trunk and back seat filled with packages. It took them a half hour just carrying the bags in the trailer. Nothing bonds women better than shopping. Especially a whole afternoon of shopping. They were already the best of friends. My wife had turned on the water heater and she told me later she almost had to force her into the shower. Once she got her in, she couldn't get her out. She stayed in there almost an hour. She had washed her hair twice, and just stood in there letting the water run over her.

I had checked the propane and there was gas. I turned on one tank and left the other one closed. I had lit the stove in the kitchen, so I knew it was working. My wife came out and said she is getting dressed. I have never seen anyone this excited except kids on Christmas morning. I said this is her first Christmas morning. She said I went a little over the five hundred, I put about two hundred on the credit card.

Jean came out wearing her clothes as if she was in a fashion show. She had a wide smile and kept looking down at her cowboy boots as she walked. I said you didn't find those at Goodwill. My wife said no, but she really wanted them. She said I can't get her to sit down in the trailer, she is afraid she will get it dirty.

I said I didn't check to see if the beds had sheets and blankets. Check and if they don't take her down and buy some. She went back in and checked. She said there were sheets on the bunks and another set in a drawer. The problem is going to be getting her to sleep in them.

This had been a lot of fun and made me feel good on every level. But now I have to go back to work. I have depleted a lot of my cash. Today was Friday and I would get back in the grove tonight at the auction. I went to the sale a little early to get a parking place and to talk to the owner. A few months ago, I had stopped at a little auction in Banning. I had run into a guy I hadn't seen in three or four years. He had brought a load of mustangs to the sale. He told me he was living in Wickiup Arizona and had brought this bunch of mustangs he had traded from the Indians. He traded all kinds of things to them and took mustangs in exchange. He said he usually ended up with about fifteen or twenty a month. He took them around to different auctions because you couldn't sell too many in one spot. He said that they averaged about twenty-five dollars ahead after commissions and everything. He allowed the Indians five dollars a head in trade, and figured he was making twenty dollars per horse. I took his phone number and told him I would give him a call.

I wanted to talk with Dave about the mustangs. I wanted to know if there was any market for them. I caught him on his way to the sale barn. He stopped and talked to me for twenty minutes or so. He told me that both of his contracts called for eight-hundred pounds or better. One of the contracts wouldn't take them if they were under that and the other one would take them at half price. I asked how much if I brought fifteen or twenty every month, He said fifty dollars. I said, I'll see what I can do. It was a pretty good sale night. There must not be much going on. Everyone had come to the sale to visit. There was a large crowd and a lot of people I hadn't seen in a long time. There was also a lot of horses. I think a lot of summer camp horses were here. I was visiting and talking with old friends until nearly midnight. I had picked up a couple of leads that might make a few dollars.

I called Johnny in Wickiup. If you can deliver twenty head a month to El Monte, I will pay thirty dollars a head. Foals or yearlings don't count. I had asked Dave what day of the month he wanted them on, and he said the twentieth would be about right. Johnny asked for the day and I said the twentieth of every month. He said it's a deal. I didn't know how long it would be before I was cut out of the deal. Four hundred a month for nothing, was good even if it only lasted a month or two.

I had a strange call from someone I didn't know. Someone introduced herself as Janet Morris. She asked what I would charge to pick up a mare and foal in Lexington Kentucky and deliver them to her farm in Solvang? I said that is a pair that take a lot of extra care. I wouldn't make a trip like that for less than two thousand dollars. She didn't even think it over. She asked when I could go? I asked if in the morning was soon enough? She said I was told you were a little cocky, but very good. The farm where they are is Sweet Grass Farm, the address is two thousand Paris Pike, Lexington. I'll tell them you are coming. Where do I deliver them? Rolling Meadows Farm Eighteen Old Stone Road Solvang. See you in a few days.

I called the trailer manufacturer in Oklahoma City and ordered a four-horse trailer with a removable center divider, and a floor mat. I needed to give them enough room to be together, and I didn't want the floor to be slick. My trailer and most trailers have a solid center divider, that will swing but it won't come out. I put a few cloths in my travel bag, and told my wife to keep an eye on Jean and I hit the road. I stopped in Phoenix for a hamburger, and I stopped in Albuquerque for an early breakfast. I pulled into a rest stop and slept for two hours. I had an early lunch in Amarillo. I had to really hurry to get to Oklahoma City before they closed. If I was too late, I would have to spend the night. I barely made it. They close at five and I pulled in the gate at four thirty. I paid, and hooked up and back on the road by five. I staid on the forty until I hit the sixty-five. I turned north to Elizabeth Town and headed east to Lexington I could load today but I decided I should get a night's sleep. The trip home was going to be tough. I checked into the Best Western and watched Television for a while before I went to sleep.

I had breakfast at six and was at the farm by seven. I had already moved the divider so I was ready to load. They brought out the mare and foal, and the guy who seemed to be in charge said load the mare and the foal will follow. I said stop right there. This guy doesn't know what he is talking about. Get hands on that foal and carry him into the trailer. The mare will follow him in but the foal will not follow her in. He will panic and be running all over this ranch looking for her. The guy said how many pairs have you hauled? Evidently a lot more than you. He said it's his responsibility, do it his way. They caught the foal and carried him and the mare walked right in with her nose touching him all the way. I closed the trailer, and went in the side door and tied her in with enough slack for her to turn her head and watch him but not enough for her to turn around and maybe step on him. I hung a hay net in her manger so she had something to fool with. I said thanks guys, and I noticed the boss had left the area. I drove out of the gate slowly giving them a chance to adjust to the motion. In an hour both of them will have their sea legs and will be rock solid.

The only difference hauling these was the stops were for a little more time to give the foal a chance to nurse. I watered the mare on the same three-hour schedule, but I stayed an extra ten or fifteen minutes. The trip was so smooth it was spooky. I slept a couple of hours in the mornings and a couple of hours in the evening. I made Solvang about midnight. I pulled in and put my seat back and went to sleep. I was awakened about daylight by some one knocking on my window. I rolled down the window and he said do you have a mare and foal in there? I said I do. He said is everything ok? I said every thing is perfect. He said I didn't expect you for a couple of days yet. I said, you know how it is. Time is money. He said I'll get some help. I said do you have a stall for them? He said yes. I said we don't need any help. I took him around and showed him how to open the trailer. I'll go inside and when I'm ready you can open the back. I went in and put a lead rope on the mare and unhooked her. I told him to open the back. He un latched it and I unloaded the mare and the foal followed her out. The guy led the way to where they were going to put them. It turned out to be a small paddock with a shelter in it. I liked it. It had the best part of a pasture and a stall. When I led the mare in and took the lead rope off, she trotted a little to loosen up, I guess. The colt of course jumped and bucked a few steps. After he had figured out his boundaries he would run and play.

I went back and was locking the back when a lady who I knew was the boss by her man's attitude came walking over. She said have you got my baby in there? I said no mam, he is in the paddock over there. She gave me a look that I couldn't translate, and walked out toward the paddock. I was in limbo here. I thought it would be rude to just drive away, and yet I wasn't going to stand around here very long. She went in the paddock and walked around the mare and foal as if inspecting for damage. I decide to give her ten more minutes and I was a ghost. I looked at my watch and fully intended to drive away in exactly ten minutes. She had one more minute left when she came out of the paddock and started my way.

She said, "would you like to come up to the house for a drink?"

"It's a little early for me and I need to get back to the farm."

"The breeding foreman called me and complained about you. He said you were rude. No actually he said you were an arrogant prick."

I smiled and said, "I don't have patience for people with authority, that don't know what they are doing."

"Is that what you thought of him?"

"One hundred percent fake. He may not even know which end of a horse the hay goes in."

She said, "I have to agree with you. I have known him a long time. He is my brother."

I said, "oops."
She said, "when you are right, you are right. What I want to talk to you about is I have reports that you seemed to have a knack for finding well-bred mares for reasonable prices. I could use five or six mares that fit that description."

"I have your number and if I find a few mares, I will

give you a call."

She said, "at least come up to the house and get your check."

I walked with her and we didn't have anything in common to talk about.

We went in and she picked up my check and handed it to me. The house was furnished with taste. She may have paid someone to do it. If she did it herself, she had a good eye. Just to make conversation I asked, "how many mares do you have now?"

She said, "I have fifteen, but there is a problem. I took some advice from a blood stock agent before I had started to study blood lines. I way overpaid for mares that have very little value. I don't know what to do now."

"The agent wasn't by any chance named Benson, was he?"

"You know him?"

"Everyone in the horse business, for any length of time knows him. I call him the maker of broken dreams. Give me a list of your mares and let me see if there is anything to be salvaged."

She went to her computer and printed me a list. The list had the price she had paid for each horse and it made me wince. I told her, "I would take a look and give her a call in two or three days."

She walked me to the door and shook my hand. I went

on my way.

I reached home about noon and unhooked the trailer. I went over to the stable and my wife was over there showing Jean how to cook on her stove. I knocked on the door and Jean came and let me in. My wife said did you tell him. Jean turned to me and said we made three hundred and eighty dollars over the weekend. Wow Jean you are going to make us all rich. That is great.

I asked Billy if there was anything, we needed to do for the business end of it. He said we needed to make an area for these kids to hang out in. They were wandering all over the place and he was afraid one of them was going to get hurt. I said pick out a place and we will build a people corral just the way we built the horse corral.

I was checking out Janet's mares and the phone rang. It was Clay Roberts. The guy that I had bought horses from because he was in trouble at the bank. He said he was going to need to sell two more of his mares. Was I interested? I told him I was always interested in a horse that had a little profit in it. He gave me the names of the two mares and told me he was asking ten thousand each. I told him I would look them up and get back to him this afternoon. I finished checking out Janet's mares.

I had put my price estimate of each mare as I looked them up. There were two big surprises. Two of the mares turned out to be what he had represented them all to be. Except for those two mares he had sold her five thousand-dollar mares for fifteen to twenty thousand dollars apiece. Those two mares, besides being much better bred than the others were both big time producers. I can't think of any reason for him to put those mares in the group unless he didn't know anything about breeding at all. I called Janet and asked if she had time to talk to me. She did, and I told her the bad news. He had robbed her but being the dummy that he is he had outsmarted himself. I told her she had two mares that might pay for the entire bunch. The one mare was sired by a successful son of Bold Ruler and had a son that had won over a million dollars. The other mare was by Swaps and had a son that had won almost three million dollars.

She interrupted me to tell me that is the mare you just brought home. I told her that those two mares in foal, in the Keenland fall sale, might bring two or three hundred thousand dollars each. She asked what should she do with the others. I told her to put them in the Hollywood Park sale and cross her fingers. She asked if I could sell them for her. I said I would give the breeding to anyone that came around looking for mares. I didn't want to try to outright sell them. She said I can understand that. You need to uphold your reputation.

When we ended the call, I turned to my computer and looked up the mares that Clay needed to sell. They both had decent breeding and if they looked alright should sell for ten or twelve thousand. I had to buy them for eight thousand or there was nothing in it for me. I called him and told him he was on the money with the price he had on the mares. I told him I wouldn't make an offer without seeing them, but I couldn't give more than eight thousand for each of them. I had to make a profit or there was no point of my buying them. I am not a breeder. I just buy and sell. If he was willing to take eight thousand, I would come out and look. He said he would talk it over with his wife and get back to me.

He called back in about an hour and said to come look at the mares. My wife had put the new trailer on Craigslist and I didn't want to dirty it. I hooked up my six-horse and drove out there. I looked at the mares and they both were nice mares. I guess they had decided that sixteen thousand wasn't going to make them well. He asked if I was willing to buy one more mare for the same price. He let me look at her papers. She had pretty good breeding and had won six races. I told him I would take her. I must have had a premonition because I had stopped at the bank and drawn out thirty thousand dollars. I loaded the mares and came on home. His ranch didn't have much grass because he was in a spot where you only had grass if you irrigated it. When I turned the mares in the paddock with ankle deep grass. They rolled in it and went to grazing. At least I had something to sell.

At breakfast my wife told me someone was coming to look at the trailer at ten o'clock. I had to hang around to meet him. I went out to look at the mares to see if they needed any hair clipping. One of them was a little shaggy around her feet. I got a lead rope and a pair of hand clippers, and took care of it.

The guy showed up about nine-thirty. This particular model of trailer I usually paid fourteen hundred for and sold them for nineteen hundred. This time they had charged me a hundred for the floor mat, so I wanted to get two thousand. I asked for twenty-two, expecting him to offer less, and instead he paid me. As I was getting the paperwork for him, he told me he had looked at the same trailer, and the dealer asked thirty-six hundred. I had never priced them at a dealer, and now I understand why I never have any trouble selling my trailers.

I answered my phone and it was Phillip Roth, a horse trader from San Francisco. He said he was on the road with a load of horses, and would make my area about two o'clock. He was calling me because he had four nice Quarter Horses on the trailer. They were too nice to take to the auction. He wanted to know if I was interested. I asked how much, and he said if I took all four, he would take six-hundred each. I told him to come by and I would take a look. He had never been to my place, so I gave him the address. He drove in about two-thirty. He had a long cattle trailer. By head and tailing the horses you could get ten head on it, and he had it full. He had the Quarter horses on the back and we unloaded them. I looked at each horse, judging his conformation. All four were handsome and well made. I asked if they were broke to ride. He told me that all four were broke, but they didn't know a whole lot. I liked them and asked if he could get along on five hundred? He said the best he could do was five-fifty. I agreed and we put them in box stalls. I gave him twenty-two-hundred and he gave me the papers. He said from time to time I run across a nice horse. If you are in the market for better horses, I'll start putting them on the trailer. I told him that I liked thoroughbreds best, but I was always in the market for nice horses.

After he left, I called a friend of mine who was a trainer. His thing was to go to Oklahoma or Texas, and buy nice young Quarter Horses. He would bring them back and make performance horses of them and sell them. When he was finished with a horse, he was fine tuned to the max. But if you bought one of his horses you were going to pay five or six thousand dollars. He wanted to be paid for his work.

His wife answered the phone and told me he was working a horse and she would have him call me when he came in. I drove over to the stable to see what was going on. Billy had picked a spot for our people corral and was clearing brush and trash out of the space. I liked the location and let him continue his job.

My wife was in the house with Jean and I knocked on the door. Jean came to the door and let me in. I asked how things are going and my wife told me Jean had spent her first night in her new home. I said that's great. I think she should make the total move. I'll clean out the house and paint the inside and make it look decent for kids to use the rest room in there. My wife thought that was a terrific Idea. I asked Jean if the bed was comfortable and she smiled and said yes.

I went out to talk to Billy. I told him I had the Quarter Horses and I wanted him to bring one at a time over here and put some training on them just like he did with the Thoroughbred geldings. I told him we were going to make the house a restroom. He said he thought that was great. My phone rang and it was Bobby, the trainer. I told him I had two three-year olds and two four-year olds that he should come take a look at. He asked how much? I told him eight hundred each. He paid more than that for the horses he was buying in the country and had the expenses of the buying trip. He said he would come by in the morning.

I saw Jean and my wife moving stuff from the house to the trailer. I told my wife to let me know when they were finished. She said there is not much to move, they should be done in a few minutes. Three horses came back from a ride. Billy took the horses and one of the girls called her mom to come pick them up. Things were settling into a regular routine. It was going to be ok.

I emailed Janet the breeding of the three mares from Clay. I put a price of ten thousand each on them. I told her these were the best I had right now. The phone rang and I thought it would be Janet, and it was Barbara from Texas. I told her she caught me by surprise. I was expecting a call from someone else.

She said, "I have a question. Would you drive this far for just four mares?"

"I don't measure a deal in miles. I measure it in profits. What do you have for me?"

"I am so angry with my father I can't think straight. He came to my barn yesterday and counted my mares himself. He then told me that he had said I must reduce my mares by twenty. He claimed I had been lying to him for six months, and he was making it very clear, that if I had not sold those last mares by the end of the week, he was shutting me down permanently. I have never seen my dad so mad. I was afraid he was going to have a heart attack. I can't believe he would get that worked up over four horses."

"He may have been mad about his daughter telling him the same lie for months. The horses may not have anything to do with it. What is it you want to do?"

She said, "I just emailed the breeding. Two of the mares I don't want to sell. They have to be off the ranch by the end of the week. I could take them to a friend's place, but if he ever found out, I might be disowned. He was really mad."

"How much are these mares going to cost me?"

"You will see these are really nice mares. I don't want to sell them but I have no choice. I gave twenty thousand for one of these mares and twenty-five for the other one. I am going to sell them to you for ten thousand apiece if you are here by Friday. I will sell the other two for eight thousand each. I will make sure it cost my dad some of his money."

"Give me twenty minutes to look at them, and I will call you back."

I pulled up the mares and they were the best that she had sold me to date. I would buy these mares even if I didn't have any customers. I texted her that I was on my way. The bad thing was I couldn't leave now because Bobby was coming to look at the Quarter horses in the morning. I hooked up my trailer, and put my travel bag in the truck. I was ready to go the minute Bobby was finished looking at the horses. My wife came home from Jeans place and I listened to her account of her day. It would be comical if it wasn't so real and so personal. I should be writing some of these things down. It might make a hell of a movie one day. Someone like Lucile Ball could turn this into a side-splitting show.

I was at the barn by seven and hoped that Bobby wasn't a late riser. I breathed a sigh of relief when he drove in about seven-thirty with his trailer hooked on. I took the horses out one at a time. He looked at them with an experienced eye. He knew what he was looking for. When he had finished looking, he said he would take the two four-year olds. He said he liked them all but he was already working two and he didn't have time for six. If I still had them when he moved a couple, he would come back. I told him I would open a vein if I had a horse that long. He wrote me a check. I gave him the papers, and helped him load the horses. He pulled out and I was right behind him. I got on the interstate and set my cruise control right on the speed limit and never backed off of it until Texas. I stopped for gas and a hamburger and didn't ease up again, until I was at Barbara's place. Thirty hours was a pretty good time. I had called her when I was about thirty miles out to let her know where I was.

She was waiting for me when I arrived. I gave her the money in cash, and she wrote me a receipt in case I ran into a brand inspector. The papers went into the glove compartment and I was back on the road in less than an hour. She told me she really hated letting these mares go. She was down to her keeping mares and didn't want to lose any of them. I told her to make peace with her father and maybe she wouldn't lose any more. I told her she had my number if there was ever anything else, I could do for her, and I had enjoyed doing business with her.

I had hung the hay nets and thought I wouldn't need to water them until the first three hour stop. I was going to sleep a couple of hours at that stop, if it has cooled off enough to sleep. I wasn't trying to get home in thirty hours. There was plenty of time to amble home. It took forty-eight hours to get home because I had to water the horses and I took three sleep breaks. A two-hour nap keeps me on the road. One of them I cheated on and slept three hours.

I pulled in at the ranch well before dark. I turned the mares in with the other three. It was a large paddock, and they would settle in an hour or so. I walked up to the house. I was too tired to unhook the trailer. My wife wasn't home and I didn't know if that was good or bad. I called her on the phone and she said she was just leaving and would be home in twenty minutes. When she came in, she said she was still having to keep an eye on Jean. She was having some trouble learning how the appliances worked. She was as tired as I was. I suggested we go out to eat. She liked the idea and we went to Red Robbin because we liked their onion rings. We talked about Jean, and she didn't think Jean was improving. She didn't seem to retain any of the things we were trying to show her. I am afraid she will burn the place down. What will happen if you stay away a couple of days. It will force her to pay attention to what she is doing. Ok but if she burns the place down it is not my fault. We went home and went to bed. I woke up in the morning still thinking about Jean.

At breakfast I said what do you think about finding a lady that needs a place to live and have her move in with Jean. There are two beds and two could live there comfortably. My wife thought about it for ten minutes and finally said that is a good idea but we will have to pick her carefully. She can't be so old she needs care herself. Why don't you go down to day and talk to the people that run the women's shelter? They might know someone trust worthy, who needs a place to live. She said that is also a good idea. Did you lay awake all-night thinking about this? No. it came to me in a dream. She said you are so full of it.

I went to the office and emailed Janet the breeding. I priced the two best mares at thirteen thousand, and the other two at ten thousand. I unhooked the trailer and went to the stable. Jean was saddling the three horses she was going to tie out front. I said, "let me ask you a question. If I could find a nice gal about your age. Would you like to have company? She would know how to operate all of the things in the trailer and you would have a friend to talk to at night."

She said, "what about your wife?"

I said, "she can't come every day. She has her own house to take care of. She can't be here at night so there is no one to talk to."

"I never had a friend, and it might be fun. If we don't like each other and she is mean to me can I ask her to leave?"

"Of course, it is your home."

"When will I get to meet her?"

"In a few days."

I was saved from a lot of questions when two ladies

came to rent horses.

I walked over to the people corral. He had two corner post holes dug. I measured them and they were good. I went out to the poles with the chain saw and cut eight post eight feet long. By the time I had done that Billy had come to work. We had discovered that a bow saw was easier to control cutting vees in the top of the post. Billy and I muscled two of the post around and set then in the holes he had dug. I started cutting vees while he went back to digging holes. I cut a vee in both tops in the same time he dug a hole. I told him one hole a day was plenty. There was no point in breaking our backs. I drug one of the poles around with the truck. We rolled it over to the post and we muscled it up one end at a time. I put the level on it and it was so close to level that I wasn't going to fool with it. We tamped the poles good with a level on the side to keep them straight. I would chain the poles down last in case we needed to make some adjustments.

I went home and hooked up my flat bed trailer. I needed three more poles and I only had two. If I was going, I might as well get two each trip. I went over to the yard and they loaded me up. I unloaded the poles where we were going to use them. I went in the house to see what was left there. There was an old sofa, a small table and two old chairs. The bedroom had two old beds with a sagging mattress. I decided that it would haul better in my horse trailer. I took the flatbed home and traded it for the horse trailer.

I told Jean I was going to throw the sofa and bed away. I did that in case she had something hidden in one or the other. She said they were no good. I looked closely at the sofa in case Joe had hid something in it. Billy and I loaded everything in the horse trailer. We went to the dump and dropped it off.

I unhooked my trailer and had my wife go with me to pick out paint. We decided on a real light tan and a brown for trim. I bought a new toilet seat and rollers and brushes. I asked if they had a sign that said restroom. I was surprised to find that they had one. I bought a toilet paper holder and a package of toilet paper. Tomorrow was clean up the house day. I had asked if they had a latch that put a sign out side that said in use. They didn't have anything like that. I decided that I would put a good lock on the door and hang one key attached to a little board that said rest room. If the key was gone the restroom was in use. We started early in the morning and had the entire inside painted by one o'clock. We replaced the toilet seat and hung a toilet paper holder. We put the restroom sign out side and we were in business.

My wife left to pick up a lady that had agreed to live with Jean. She said she had talked to four different women, and this one sounded like she would get along with Jean. She was gone a couple of hours and I thought maybe the lady had changed her mind. She finally came driving in. She took the lady inside to introduce her to Jean. I left that up to the women to make everything mesh. She had introduced her to me as Sally Watts. She seemed like a level headed lady, and she was neat and clean. Her cloths were old but clean. My wife was in there so long I was seeing disaster. She came out after two hours and said it might work. They are both shy so it could take a while. At least Sally knows how everything works. I left them watching television. I hope they bond.

I asked what is the deal with this lady. My wife said she went through a divorce about five years ago. Her husband was a career solider and she had never worked because they lived all over the world. He was paying her alimony. She said it wasn't much but she could live on it. He got remarried and he died two years ago. His new wife got everything and the alimony stopped. She has no work experience and can't find a job. She lives on a couple of part time jobs. I hope for both of their sakes they get along.

I don't know why, but I took my phone out of my pocket and looked at it. I had two missed calls and I hadn't heard a thing. The first call was from Bobby the Quarter horse trainer. I called him and he told me he had a customer for the other two Quarter Horses. He was sending him over to look at them. He should be there about one o'clock. I looked at my watch and it was ten to one. I jumped in the truck and tore over to the ranch. I pulled into the drive and I saw a truck parked at the barn, he was already here. I parked next to his truck and one of the Mexicans had a horse out of the stall showing him. I walked over and the guy turned to me and said, "hello, I am Rick Mendoza, I hope you don't mind me looking at your horses without you."

"No, I don't mind. Go right on."

He said something in Spanish, and my guy led the horse away from him. He said something else and he trotted him back. He spoke to him again and he put the horse away and brought out the other one. He walked around looking at every angle, and then he had him go through the walk and trot routine. He had him put the horse away. He turned to me and said, "they are nice horses. Bobby said they would be around a thousand, is that so?"

"They are close to a thousand. I want eight hundred apiece for them."

He looked me in the eye and said, "I think I will buy both of them."

"Fine, come in the office and I'll get their papers. I asked, how he knew Bobby?"

"I have known Bobby for many years. I have bought several horses from him over the years. He has well trained horses."

"You know these horses are just broke, and haven't any schooling, right?"

"Yes, I know that. I have a different use for these horses. Will a check be ok with you?"

"It will be fine. When will you pick them up?"

"My son is loading a horse at Bobbies, and will be along any minute."

He gave me a check and he gave me his card and said, "keep my card we may do more business in the future. Are those mares in the pasture?"

"They are Thoroughbred mares, but I am not a breeder. I buy and sell."

"We will for sure do more business in the future. I do the same thing. I buy and sell."

Just then an expensive horse van pulled in the drive. Rick went out to wave him back where we were. We loaded the horses and Rick introduced me to his son. They both shook my hand and he said something to my guy that had the word gracias in it and drove away.

I still had another call on my phone. It was Janet and she said I will take two of those mares and gave me the names. Anytime you can get away, bring them on up. I said I will bring them in the morning. And she said I'll be looking for you.

Why couldn't all sales be like those two were. They knew what they wanted to do, and did it. My kind of people. I went back to the stable. I needed to get things cleaned up for the weekend. Billy was digging another hole and was nearly finished. As soon as he was finished, we pulled the post over there and stood them in the two holes. He started on another hole while I cut the vees in the top of the post. When I had the vees cut, we rolled the poles over and muscled them one end at a time, up on the post. I put the level on the pole and one end had to have a little dirt under the post to make it level. I had a six-foot iron bar with one end sharpened into a point, I drove the point into the post at ground level and put a brick under it as the pivot and pushed the end of the bar down to pry the post up. It worked like a charm and Billy pushed some dirt under the post and it was level. We repeated the process on the other side and it was near dark. We had three sides up and I didn't want any digging of holes or lifting of poles with kids around I told Billy we would finish it on Monday. In the afternoon my wife had come over to see how the girls were doing. She didn't stay very long and I took that to be a good sign. I didn't ask her how they were doing until we got home. She said they seemed to be getting along. We had to wait and see if they started getting on each other's nerves later on.

I told Billy that I had to deliver a couple of horses and would be gone. I wanted him to be involved in the horse rental all day. I told him that since Sally was new, I didn't want her handling horses or money. I hooked up my trailer and had it ready to go for the morning. I loaded the mares and was on the road by seven. I would be there about noon.

I drove up her drive at exactly twelve o'clock. She must have been watching for me because she came out of the house when I started up the drive. She reached the barn at the same time I did. She stood back while I unloaded the mares. They were both grand looking mares. She wouldn't be disappointed by their looks. Her guys had put their lead shanks on them and stopped for her to look them over. They went to turn them out in a paddock and she invited me to the house. We went in the house and she served me lemon aid. We sat down and she said, "I would have had you bring the other mares but I need to get my mares under control. I have twelve mares I need to find a home for. It goes without saying I am going to take a huge loss no matter what I do. I have talked to twenty different people and none of them are willing to try helping me disperse these horses."

"You have two options. You can take these horses to auction and take what ever they bring. Or you can donate them to some charity and write off whatever you paid for them. You should not be talking to horsemen. You should be talking to a tax specialist."

"I can't believe that no one has mentioned that to me. Are you the only one in this business that knows anything about it?"

"This business is very deceptive. It looks so simple, and everyone thinks they can do it. The truth is, it is very complicated. In my thirty years in it, I have seen a hundred people go broke. Either they go broke, or they cause someone they talked into investing to go broke. There are so many ways to go broke with horses. There are few ways to make money with horses. There are two kinds of people that will always cause failure if you listen to their advice. One is an out and out crook like you got hooked up with. The other is the guy who tells you he is an expert and doesn't know zip.

The racing commissions around the country have not made any effort to regulate the people that are involved in racing, but are not at the race track. They don't seem to realize they should be regulating everything that pertains to racing. They allow people to form syndicates and take investors to race horses who know nothing about racing. They are promoters not racing people. Racing commissions are made up of people that are friends or campaign contributors of the Governor. They should be appointed by a horsemen's committee. The newly elected Kentucky Governor appointed a new racing commission. Not one person on that Commission has ever owned a horse of any kind. It is their job to write all of the rules for racing when they don't know a thing about it. The racing commissions all over the country are ruining racing. They have allowed anyone that applies for a trainer's license to have one. To show you what is wrong with that, I will tell you a story of an event I watch unfold.

"I was at a race track in Indiana working as a racing official. We had a young guy come to the track with a couple of horses. He applied for a trainer's license and they gave it to him. They race at night there, and one night after the races my wife and I were having diner in a café by the track. There was an older couple at the table next to us that had been to the races. One of them said that was fun I wonder if we should get a horse. Out of nowhere this kid appeared and sat down with them and started telling them how he would win the Kentucky Derby for them. My wife was the claims clerk at the time and the next thing you know they had deposited three hundred thousand dollars in the office for him to claim horses with. He spent the whole three hundred thousand and never won one race for them. That is happening all over this country."

She said, "I can't believe they let that happen."

"Everyone has a little to be blamed for. In the old days to get a trainer's license you had to jump through hoops. First, you had to have worked for a trainer for a considerable time. You then went to the Stewards and asked to apply for a license. They would give you an oral exam. If you passed that, they would give you a written exam that was very detailed. If you passed that you had a barn test. You met at a barn with a trainer and a veterinarian, and a horses shoer. You had to prove to them all, that you knew everything you needed to know to train horses. If you failed to impress at any point, they told you to try again in a year. A trainer's license meant something. About nineteen eighty, a young guy came along with a horse and just expected to go out there and train his horse. They threw him off the track, and he went to court, he said they were keeping him from making a living. The Judge ruled in his favor and they had to give him a license. If anyone on the commission would have had half a brain it would have been ok. A new jockey is listed as an apprentice Jockey. He is monitored by the Stewards and can only ride proven horses. They don't become a full-fledged Jockey until they win twenty races. If they would have made the same rule for trainers, everything would have been ok. A lot of those guys won't win twenty races in their life time. But no one thought of it."

She said, "is it not possible to make that change retro-active?"

"You would never get it done now."

"What would you do with my horses, if you were me.?"

You are asking me a specific question. That means I have to give you a specific answer. I would get them off my feed bill as soon as possible. They are cost-ing you five or six hundred dollars a month in feed. I would sell them for whatever I could get for them. If I needed the money, I would put one or both of the good mares in the sale at Keenland. If I didn't need the money, I would keep the two mares and breed them to a good stud and sell their yearlings at Keenland."

"What will the mares I need to get rid of bring at a local horse auction?"

"I bought two nice mares a couple of months ago. To get the two mares, I had to buy a third mare which was about the same caliber as several of your mares.

I put her in the auction at El Monte and she brought four hundred and twenty-five dollars."

"In other words, I am going to lose two or three hundred thousand?"

"That would be the case if he didn't let those two mares fall through a crack in his scheme. As it is, you are just breaking even. Your tax man may be able to make it profitable."

"I will ask another specific question. Will you help me sell these mares at an auction? I have never been to a horse auction in my life."

"How many are you going to sell?"

"I think I should sell all twelve of the duds. Don't you agree they should all go?"
"Let me talk to Tom Caldwell. He is an auctioneer at Keenland and see what he thinks we should do. I'll call you after I talk to him. I will help you put them through an auction if he agrees that is best."

On the way home I racked my brain looking for a market for her mares. It hadn't come to me yet. I didn't feel like unhooking the trailer. I just parked and walked to the house. My wife said they had a pretty good day at the stable. They had done almost five hundred dollars. I went to bed early.

Sunday morning, I went to the stable to see what was going on. Billy had put a dozen hay bales in our three-sided corral for seats. It was a great idea and I was impressed. I asked if any of the kids had used the rest-room? He said he thinks every damn one of them had used it at least once. It was the most popular spot on the ranch.

I helped Jean and Billy saddle horses. We saddled twelve. Billy thought that would be enough. While we were saddling, I asked Jean how she liked her new roommate. She said she really liked her. She was the friend she had always wanted. I would have to re-member to thank my wife when I went home.

The first hour we were open parents dropped off nine kids. They would stop out front and let the kids out, and drive on. By eleven o'clock, we had fourteen kids hanging around. They had their ride and hung around visiting and watching. I saw what Billy meant about the rest room. There was a steady parade to the rest room. The key was never hanging on the hook for more than five minutes. The action picked up after church and we had too many kids hanging around. We had become a weekend child care center. At one point we had twenty-five kids just hanging around. I couldn't run them off because some of them had brought money for a second ride and were saving it until later. I couldn't complain. We did a little over five-hundred for the day. We didn't have anything the kids could hurt, and most of them stayed close to the front where they shouldn't get hurt. Sally came out of the house a couple of times to see what was going on, but she didn't stay long. I didn't get a chance to ask how she was doing, but she looked content.

We were starting to generate enough revenue that I need to put in place a money handling routine. I couldn't have Billy or Jean walking around with several hundred dollars in their pocket. That was asking for a disaster. I didn't want them to get hurt by some goofball trying to rob them.

I had gone to a large safe company in Los Angeles and looked at safes. They had one I liked. It had a slot in the top that you dropped the money in. I had to have a place to bolt it to the floor, that was protected from the weather. What I finally did was close off the back bedroom in the restroom house. I put a door in the back wall by the trailer. Anyone trying to break in that door would be heard in the trailer, I bolted the safe to the floor and we were in business. Every time they collected a hundred or so, they could come in and drop it in the safe. I felt better about it then.

I called my friend that was in the Quarter horse business and talked to him about Janet's mares. I asked if he knew a Quarter horse man that would like some Thoroughbred mares to breed to his stud. He said he would ask around. Some guys might be interested. He would give me a call.

I called Tom Caldwell and talked to him about Janet's problem. He agreed with me that she was better off unloading them as soon as possible. He said the Hollywood auction would be the best place to sell them. Their auction was coming up in six weeks, and she needed to enter them now so they would be in the catalog. I called Janet and told her what he said. She said she would enter them as soon as I hung up.

One day I was driving through the industrial section of Van Nuys looking for a place a guy had told me had some metal vats that would make great water troughs. I saw sitting in a company yard, two little buildings that looked like ticket booths. I turned around and went back to look at them. That's what they were and I asked if they were for sale. The guy went in to ask someone and ended up getting sent from person to person before he finally found someone who said I could buy one for eight hundred dollars. I wrote him a check and went home for my flat bed trailer. They loaded it with a fork lift. I worried all the way home, how I was going to get it off the trailer without tearing it up. We took an hour to decide where to put it. I didn't want it seen from the street. I didn't want the place to look too commercial from the street. We finally decided to put it next to the restroom. Billy had his friends come over to help us.

I set up to unload it far enough away from the building that if it tipped over, we wouldn't wreck both buildings. I had two metal ramps that came with trailer to load a car with. They had hooks that fit over the edge of the trailer. The problem is they were very steep, and I was afraid the building would tip over. My trailer had a winch on the front, and I planned to use that to control the decent of the booth. I put wide nylon straps around the booth high up near the roof.

I tightened the ratchet until the strap was snug and then attached the cable from the winch to it. We had to move it about four feet before we got to the ramp so we had a chance try my idea before we went over the edge. We tested it by giving the cable just a little slack and moving the booth till it took the slack. I realized that I had not thought it through. When we pushed it over the edge and the bottom started to slide with the top secured it was going to pull it over backwards. I added another nylon strap at the bottom to make it evenly secured. We inched it forward a foot at a time and finally reached the ramp. This was the moment of truth. We gave it a little slack and pushed it on the ramp. It wasn't far enough to tip yet. We gave it a little more slack, and pushed again. This time it tipped and slid about two feet before the winch stopped it. I thought we had lost it but we had it under control now. We slowly let off on the winch and the booth moved down the ramp. When the edge of the booth reached the ground, I unhooked the winch and slowly drove the truck away to pull the ramps from under the building. Once it was sitting on the ground, every one took a big breath of relief. I had bought concrete paver to set the booth on. Once we had skidded it into place, we tipped it from side to side and put the pavers under it. A job well done. I gave Billy's friends thirty bucks apiece, and asked if they wanted to come tomorrow to dig some more holes? They said they would, and went home.

I bought a fancy bar stool with a back on it, and well

padded, and put it in for jean to sit on. She climbed up in there and she had found a home. She thought she was the Queen of Sheba.

The next day I staked out the rest of the holes for the perimeter fence. I talked to Billy about benches inside the corral. I said we could set pole sections in the ground for legs and put boards on top for seating. He agreed that would be a good fix, but he thought the hay bales gave it more of a country feel. We were feeding the hay every night after using it for seating so, it didn't get old. I said fine, we could always put in benches if we got tired of moving hay around.

I went back the next day looking for the water troughs. I drove around in that area for an hour, and was ready to give up when I saw them. It looked like used section of Tractor Supply. I pulled in and looked around. I bought two round water troughs. What I liked better was the hay racks he had. They were iron with bars in front and were made to hang on the wall. They would hold enough hay for one horse for the day. They looked brand new, and he had twenty-five of them. He asked ten dollars and I bought them all. The hay nets I am using now, take too long to fill, and they don't last but a few months. He had three soda machines that used cans. I asked if they work and he assured me they did. He wanted five hundred apiece for them. I thought about it all day and decided I would go back tomorrow and get one.

I had to go home for my flatbed trailer again. I ended

up with a problem, trying to tie the feeders in a safe and secure way. It took me an hour to get everything tied down. I went back to the barn and we put the round water troughs in the center of the big paddock. They were large enough to water the entire herd. It took an hour to fill each tank. The feeders were a little trickier. I put them on the stud we had nailed up to hang the nets from. I was afraid that was too narrow and they would tear them off the wall if the horse pushed hard on one side or used it as a rub bar. We put them up, and if they tore them down, we would have to get a wider board behind them.

Janet called to tell me she had entered twelve horses in the auction. She said the auction was the fifteen and sixteenth of next month. They told her that the horses couldn't come in until the fourteenth. I would have to make two loads in one day. I decided that the only way to do that would be, to bring one load to my place and leave them over night so I didn't have to go far for the second load. I told her to have them all trimmed up as if she was going to a horse show. I drove to Griffith Park and scouted around to find two girls to show the horses on the sale days. I found one girl that I knew and her girlfriend that I didn't know. I gave them the barn number, and told them to be there on the fourteenth.

I put the mares that I had left on the email broadcast and sent it. It created interest before, and maybe it would again.

The rest room house had a porch and I bored a hole in the wall to run wire through. I installed a plug and took my horse trailer to get the machine. I could tie it to the wall of the trailer so it wouldn't turn over. I brought it back and Billy and I muscled it up on the porch. The guy had machines with three different logos on them. I took the one that had Coca Cola on it. It had the best paint job and was bright. It would handle seven different sodas. After we set it up, and plugged it in to make sure it worked, I went to Sam's Club to buy soda. I bought Coke, Pepsi, Dr Pepper, and Seven Up. I still had three slots open. If I got calls for something else, I would get it. I also bought a large trash can for the empties. The machine was set up to sell a soda for a dollar. That was more than enough since they cost me thirty cents.

I had my first call on the mares I had emailed the breeding on. It was a lady from Temecula. She said she was interested in two of the mares, and could she come out today to see them? I told her that she was welcome to come at any time. I explained that I had two places that I went back and forth between, and if she would give me a call before she got here, I would be sure to meet her at the ranch. About an hour later, I had another call from a guy in Loma Vista that was also interested in two of the mares. He wanted to come in the morning and I told him to call before he came, incase I had sold the ones he was interested in. I went to the ranch and checked the mares to be sure they were presentable. I didn't want any scrapes or scratches showing. They all looked good and I went in the office to wait. It was only another hour before she called to say she was in Woodland hills and would arrive in a few minutes. I told her I was at the ranch and to drive on back to the barns.

It was about twenty minutes later when a VW convertible drove in with the top down. She came back and parked in front of the office. I walked out to meet her. She was a lady of about sixty who kept herself trim and fit. She introduced herself as Kitty Baker. I gave her my name and took her out to the paddock to look at the mares. She told me she had a small farm in Tehachapi with a stud by the name of War Baron. She had one of her mares go barren and she had sold one of her mares. She was trying to find a couple of young mares, to replenish her stock.

She walked around all of the mares and looked them all over. I pointed out the two mares she was interested in. I asked her if she sold her mares on a regular basis? She said that she only sold mares with foals and in foal again. She said that the California Breeders Fund paid a nice price on California Bred horses that win at the track. She makes more money on breeder fees than on selling them. She works hard to get as many foals out there as possible. Both of the horses she liked the breeding on, were priced at ten thousand. She asked if I would take nine thousand each if she took both? I told her I would like to help her out, but I thought the horses were priced right. She smiled and said, I think so too. If you will deliver them, I will pay the ten. I said I would, and we went to the office. She wrote me a check and I gave her the papers. I asked her how she heard about the mares since she wasn't on my list. She told me her neighbor was on the list, and he knew she was looking for mares.

I guess she thought if there was anything wrong with the mares, I would tell her now that she had bought them. She asked why are you selling these mares? I said that is what I do. I don't breed horses. I buy and sell them. She looked a little skeptical as she said how many mares have you bought and sold in the last few months. In the last two months I have sold about forty but that is a little unusual. I sold one guy fifteen head. He is starting a farm from scratch. I sold one lady twelve, she is doing the same thing. I told her I would deliver the mares tomorrow, but I wasn't sure what time, because I had someone coming to look tomorrow. I told her I would call her with the time. I put the two mares in a box stall to keep them safe. She drove away with a wave.

I went back to the stable to see how things were going. Billy was right about the kids hanging around. I counted eight. Billy told me we might need to buy more soda. That had been a big hit with every one not just the kids. A lot of parents waited for the kids to come back and all of them went to the pop machine. We had found another use for one of the power poles. We had cleared the brush away from the street for about fifty feet. We laid down one of the poles as a curb so they didn't pull to far off the street. The parents that waited had a good parking place, and they used it. Billy said that most of the parents that waited, only did it once. When they saw that there was no threat to the kids and they were having fun they didn't wait again. I checked the pop machine and a couple of the slots were near empty. I had put half of what I bought in the first loading. I put the rest of stock in the machine. I would go over to Sam's Club after we closed and buy more soda.

Jean told me she had dropped five bundles of a hundred dollars in the safe. She counted another hundred and told me to drop it. I could see she had another sixty or seventy dollars in her drawer. We started the day with twenty dollars in small bills to make change with. We had a good day and it wasn't over yet. There was still a couple of hours left.

Jean had never mentioned her money in the bank. I asked her about it and she said she didn't know how to get it out of the bank. I got her check book and taught her how to write a check. She said she couldn't think of anything she needed it for. At the end of the month I showed her our expenses and our profit of six hundred dollars. I split the profit with her and you would think she had hit the lottery. It was the first month we had made a profit, but I hoped it wouldn't be the last.

I went over to buy soda and bought double this time of the two that had sold the most. I brought the cases and put them in the back room with the safe. I filled the machine and took the money out to give to Jean to put in her drawer.

I went home and took my wife to dinner at Red Robin. I was tired and went to bed as soon as we came home.

The phone woke me up at seven o'clock. It was the guy from Loma Vista. He wanted to know about the mares. I asked which mare was he interested in. I was expecting the mares to be the two mares I had just sold. I was totally wrong. He wanted two mares that I had left. I told him to come on, I still had both of them. He drove in about ten o'clock and I took him out to the paddock to look at the mares. He went around them looking at them from all angles. As I watched him, I began to suspect that he didn't have a clue what he was looking at. I finally said we should go to the office and talk about this. We went in the office and I offered him a Dr Pepper, and he turned it down. I said why don't you tell me what you are doing here.

He said, "it is something I can't tell you about. I have backed myself into a corner I may never dig out of."

I said, "why don't you tell me why you are trying to buy mares that you don't know anything about?"

"Is it that obvious?"

"Pretty much. Are you trying to buy these mares for someone else?"

"I don't know what to do. My wife and I went through

a divorce when my daughter was thirteen. My ex wife took our daughter and moved to New York. My daughter had two mares which she couldn't take with here of course. I wasn't about to feed and clean up after two horses. I sold them. My daughter just turned twenty this year. I received a letter a couple of days ago from my daughter. She told me she just finished a two-year course in animal husbandry. She wants to breed horses and is going to start with her two mares. She will be here next week."

I asked, "were the mares' adult horses when she left?"

"Yes. Her mother had given them to her when she turned ten. Her mother had been riding them for five or six years before that."

"You have no problem. The mares were about ten years old when she was ten. That would make them twenty now. That is too old to have foals. Just tell her that you will buy her two young mares that will be able to produce foals. These mares have good breeding, but you might want to let her pick out her own mares. If she doesn't know anything about breeding you need to try to talk her out of the whole idea."

He visibly relaxed and I saw a ton lift off of his shoulders. He thanked me and told me if she insisted on buying mares, he would bring her to look at these mares.

I loaded the mares going to Temecula, and I called her and told her I was on my way. It was about four o'clock when I reached her farm. It was a nice place. It was a perfect size and sanitary looking.

She came out of the house when she heard me drive in. I told her I loved her place and I hoped she would will it to me. I unloaded the horses and we turned them out in a paddock. She asked if I needed a drink of water or to go to the restroom. I told her I was in good shape, and thanked her for asking. The traffic on the interstate at this time of day was brutal going home. There was no way to speed it up. I put a Gary Moore blues album on and relaxed and listened. He was good enough to make you forget you were stuck in traffic.

I was not looking forward to my stint at Hollywood Park, but I was committed. I would honor my commitment. Who knows, it might turn out good for me. I might make some contacts that were profitable later. You never know who is going to appear at a horse event. The thirteenth finally came, and I went to Janet's farm and brought the first load of horses to my place and put them in box stalls. I went in and went to bed, but I didn't think I would go to sleep at this time of the day. My alarm woke me up at midnight, so I did go to sleep. I got dressed and went on the road. I arrived at the farm about daylight. We loaded and I headed for Hollywood Park. I pulled in before noon. Janet and the two girls I had hired were already there. We put the horses in the stalls and I went to my ranch to get the other six horses. We were all set up by five o'clock. Janet checked into a hotel, and the girls and I lived close enough to go home.

We all came in at eight in the morning I really didn't expect a lot of viewers but we were ready if anyone came. The girls checked the horses to make sure they hadn't rolled in manure or didn't have straw in their manes. I had bought lawn chairs for us to sit on. I had brought a big cooler but I had filled it with Dr Peppers. The girls all complained when they saw only Dr Peppers. Later in the day after they had a couple, they admitted they liked it. They had never tasted it before. The girl that I knew was Mary, and her friend was Rachael.

The sale started at noon so we didn't have a lot of time to worry about lookers. The girls had decided that Rachael would take the horses to the sale ring unless they were back to back. They both had come dressed in kakis and Polo shirts. They looked really sharp. In fact, they looked so sharp that three different other sellers asked me for their names and numbers so they could call them for the next sale.

We had about a dozen different lookers. It was more than I expected, and I thought maybe we would do better than I thought we would. The first horse was coming up and we would see how they were going to do. Janet had walked up to watch a few horses sell. She had never been to a horse auction and wanted to see how they did it. Rachael took our first horse up and I crossed my fingers. She brought three thousand and five hundred dollars and I was relived. I was afraid there would be no bid. That was the low mark and the rest of them brought more. The high point of our consignment, was an extremely good-looking mare that brought seven thousand two hundred. We sold eight on Saturday and four on Sunday. The average for the twelve was sixty two hundred. I paid the girls and told them that other sellers had asked for their numbers to hire them for the next sale. They went home happy. I could see that Janet had hoped for more but I had told her what to expect. I took her for drinks and tried to cheer her up.

I tried to explain that she had to cut her loses. I said that if she had kept one of those mares here is what would have happened. You would have paid a stud fee of one thousand. You would have kept the mare for a year which would be three hundred dollars. You would keep the foal for a year and a half for another four hundred dollars. That is not adding the expense of the farm and the labor salaries. You would have near in out of pocket expenses and he would go to the same sale we were at today and if you were lucky, he would bring twenty-five hundred. You made five hundred dollars for two years of your work. You could make more working at McDonalds. The up side is you can buy five or six mares that will actually make money for you.

She asked me how much she owed me, and I told her my services were free. I told her to keep me in mind when she was going to buy more mares. She said you can bet on it. I couldn't have done it without you. We all went home glad it was over.

The phone was ringing when I walked in the door. I answered and a strange voice said, "I tried to get a chance to talk to you today at the sale. You were busy helping Janet sell her horses."

"You know Janet?"

"I know her slightly. I sold her a horse about five years ago. I stopped by her barn to say hello, and she told me you were just helping her out."

"What can I do for you?"

"My name is Justin Rose, and I own a horse farm in Kentucky. I would like to meet with you and discuss a business deal. Could I drive out and talk to you tomorrow?"

"I don't see why not. Do you have my address?"

"I do. Someone who spoke highly of you gave me your card. I will see you tomorrow."

I didn't get a lot of sleep over the last couple of days. I went to bed early and got out of bed late. It wasn't late for me. I normally don't get up until eight o'clock. I had a bowl of Raisin Bran, and went to the barn. I wasn't there more than ten or fifteen minutes when a car came up the drive. A gentleman of sixty or seventy parked in front of the barn and came in the office.

He said, "Good morning. I'm Justin Rose."

"What can I do for you Mr. Rose?"

"As I told you, I have a farm in Kentucky. My wife has never become a horse lover. Because of that, she has never spent any time around the farm or the horses. I have been told that I have serious health issues. As soon as the word got around that I was sick, half a dozen horsemen started calling in an attempt to steal my broodmare band. Guys that were my friends would call and offer ten or twenty cents on the dollar for my horses. I am so disgusted with the Kentucky Hard boots, that I would give my horses away before I would let any of my good friends buy any of them."

"If you have decent horses, they will probably bring more at the Keenland auction than I can pay for them."

"There are two reasons I don't intend to do that. I do not want any of my friends to pick up a bargain on one of my horses. The stronger reason for not doing it is simple. According to my doctor, I won't be alive at sale time. I must dispose of all of my horses while I am able to do it. My wife wouldn't know Alydar from a burro. I can't leave it for her to do."

"What is it you expect me to do for you Mr. Rose? I deal in ten to twenty thousand dollar horses. I think my bankroll wouldn't buy more than one or two of your horses. As you can see, my farm is a working ranch. It is not fancy or elegant enough to show high end horses here."

"Before I pulled in this morning, I drove around and looked at you farm. Your farm has everything mine has. It might not be as shiny as mine but it is in good working order. If you were offering a mare with a pedigree of interest to me, I would not mark her less valuable because some of your fences need painting."

"We still come back to the fact that my bank roll won't allow me to play in your league."

"Let me ask you a question. If I sent you two mares worth a hundred thousand dollars each, how much would you need to make on the sale?"

"You are asking the wrong questions. If I had a customer for that kind of horse, and I called you to supply the horse, I would be happy with ten percent. If you are going to ship me twenty horses of that quality, it is a different proposition. It might take me a year to sell the twenty head and I would have considerable expense handling them. In that case I would need to charge thirty or forty percent. California horsemen think if you have a decent stallion you can get racehorses out of five hundred dollar mares. True quality mares are hard to sell in California."

"You are on the wrong thought path. I don't need your farm, I need you. Here is my proposal. I own forty two well bred and producing mares, and two well bred stallions. I have rented a farm on the outskirts of Lexington Kentucky. I would like for you to come back and take over the farm and sell my horses. I want you to move the horses to the rented farm and represent the horses as yours. I will pay you twenty percent on each sale. Actually, you will pay my estate eighty percent of each sale. I will draw up a contract moving the horses into your name. I have paid the rent on the farm for one year. If you haven't sold them all by that time, it is your problem."

"Who sets the price on each horse?"

"I have made a list of the horses and my estimate of their value. It is my opinion of their worth, and it is not binding. You are free to sell any horse at any price you feel is appropriate."

"I have so many questions that we will never finish this conversation. For example, what about the stud fees?"

"The stud fees have all been paid. The ones that are live foal, and don't produce a foal shall be refunded to my estate."

"That is fair between you and me. People buying the mares are not going to go for that. Part of the value of the mare is in that prospective foal. If the mare aborts and the stud fee is refunded to you instead of the new owner, we will be hearing from lawyers."

"You are right. I will have to change that clause."

"How many of the forty two are not in foal?"

"Three."

"Did all three foal last year?"

"One of them did not foal last year."

"That one will definitely be considered as barren. Did you reflect that in your pricing?"

"No, I did not. This is why I need you. The auctioneer Director at Keenland, told me you were the most complete horseman he ever met. That's why I'm here."

"Next question. This is basically a one year deal. If it comes to the end of the year and I still have five horses that I have not been able to sell yet, what happens? Do they revert back to your estate?"

"No, the only thing that changes is that I will not be paying the rent on the rented farm. You will have to pick up the tab for the rent or move the horses to your farm."

"Could I see the sheet with your estimates? Let me look through them a little bit." I went in the office and started looking at the list. I wanted to check his high end estimates and his low end estimates. The first high end mare was listed for three hundred thousand. She was well bred and had won almost a million dollars. She had three foals and the first was already a two year old stakes winner. She might be worth that much. The first low end mare was fair breeding, and had won a little over a hundred thousand. She had six foals. Four of them raced three winners and one stakes winner. A minor stakes, but still a stakes winner. He had her priced at fifty thousand. Maybe a little high.

I would put her at forty thousand. He at least was in the ball park. He didn't think a ten thousand dollar mare was worth fifty thousand because he owned her. "How soon would you need an answer?"

"I would think you have some time. My doctor tells me my lights will go out some time in the next sixty days."

"I have to talk to my wife. I will give you an answer in a day or two. Running things here will put a load on her. I have to be sure she feels up to it."

He said, "he had to go on home. There were several other parts of his life he had to put in order. He gave me a card with his private number, and a copy of the contract he wanted to use. He would be waiting to hear from me."

As he drove away, I added his estimates of each horse It totaled a little over eight million dollars. If he was anywhere near correct, I stood to make over a million dollars. The real benefit would be the fact it put me on the map with the big players. That alone could be worth several million dollars in the future. I didn't see a down side, and I didn't see how I could pass on the deal. I picked up all the paperwork and went to the house to talk it over with my wife. We talked it over until supper time. After supper, I sat down to carefully read the contract he had left me. It covered every problem that might arise. The only thing that needed changing, was the clause about returning the stud fee to his estate. My wife wasn't happy about being in charge for that long. She agreed with me that we couldn't afford to pass up a million dollars. I called Justin and told him that I would do the deal. I reminded him to remove the stud fee clause. I told him I would leave in the morning and should be there in two or three days. He gave me the address of the farm and told me to call when I arrived.

I made Billy the rent stable manager. I told him if he didn't get along with Jean, I would break his neck when I got back. My wife was going to do all the banking and bill paying. If he had a problem, he should take it to her. I packed clothes and gear I would need on the farm and left at daylight. I had called Mary and asked if her and Rachel would like to spend some time in Kentucky. She said they were coming out in Rachels car and would see me there. I felt like I had spent my life training for an opportunity like this.

[M1]

[M1]

ABOUT THE AUTHOR

Max Porter

We hope you have enjoyed The Impulsive Horse Trader.

Visit me at Maxporterstoryteller.com

PRAISE FOR AUTHOR

Horse racing is a nail-biting proposition--especially in the bandit-infested Old California of this tense Western. An entertaining oater that's also a subtle study in understated manliness. --Kirkus Review

- KIRKUS REVIEW

Porter dishes on the inter workings and gritty realities of horse racing. As the FBI closes in on the assassin the action hits a gallop. The tension escalates nicely, and the characters' dialogue rings true, avoiding any since of artificiality. - Kirkus Indie Review.

- KIRKUS INDIE REVIEW

BOOKS BY THIS AUTHOR

Odyssey Of A Horseman

This is the story of a horse trainer from the racetrack in Kentucky, who makes a journey through the old west in the eighteen nineties, match racing against the horsemen he meets. Match racing is a world apart from organized racing. The only rules in match racing are what you negotiate them to be. It is a world populated by semi-con men and gamblers. If you are not extremely careful it can be hazardous to your health, because some of the players are poor losers, who would rather fight than pay. Our story will furnish the reader an insight into the world of match racing, where it takes more than the best horse to be successful. It will also give you a sense of the dangers faced by a man traveling the long desolate trails of the undeveloped west. He must be on the alert at all times to protect himself and his horses from thieves and bandits. The Author understand how the game is played in both organized and unorganized racing. He was involved in match racing in California for several

years before he went to the racetrack as a trainer.
Review

Horse racing is a nail-biting proposition--especially in the bandit-infested Old California of this tense Western.

An entertaining oater that's also a subtle study in understated manliness.

--Kirkus Indie, Review

The Horseman Returns

I would like to share a story with you of the events that took place during the continuing travels of Cole Copeland, a Kentucky horse trainer. He has traveled across the country to California, match racing along the way. He now plans to match race back to Kentucky. Match racing is different from organized racing, because you never know what you are up against. Every race is not only a threat to him financially, but could be a threat to his health. Some people take being a bad loser to extremes. Cole is also faced with the dangers of traveling through bandit infested back countries. When he is twenty miles from civilization, every person he meets is a possible death threat. The threat is heightened when he is racing, because they know he is carrying cash money.

Racing To Find An Assassin

When the FBI discover a clue that leads them to be-

lieve an assassin, they have been hunting for a decade, may be a member of the racetrack community. They persuade an established trainer to take two of their agents as clients. As owners of a racehorse they are able to move freely among the horsemen in the search for their assassin. Even though the FBI makes every effort to limit his exposure to the danger involved in their man hunt, the trainer finds himself in the position of being a possible target for the assassin. As the search unfolds, you will have a rare look at the life of a professional racehorse trainer as he conducts his daily business. You will go behind the guarded gates to meet some of the colorful people that reside in this strange and protected environment. Although training racehorses may not be as glamorous as it appears, it still holds a fascination for anyone interested in horses, or horseracing. This book is dedicated to fast horses, and those who love them.

Review

Porter dishes on the inner workings and gritty realities of horse racing. As the FBI closes in on the assassin the action hits a gallop. The tension escalates nicely, and the characters' dialogue rings true, avoiding any since of artificiality. - Kirkus Indie Review.

One Good Horse

This is the story of race horse trainer Buddy Miller and the one year that changed his life forever. Buddy will navigate through the daily rigors of his life on the race track, the murder of his college friend and

moving to Kentucky to train some of the best horses he has ever had. Training racehorses is a tough profession. It takes a set of skills that not everyone possesses. It takes someone that is mentally tough enough to face defeat day in and day out because a trainer loses 80% of his races. It takes a person that is confident enough in his own abilities to make decisions in that environment.

The Dragon Maker

An FBI agent was sent from his home office in Little Rock Arkansas to Lake Havasu Arizona to investigate a drowning in the lake. He had no idea why he was sent two thousand miles to check out a drowning. He was given no information about the who or the why. The first thing he discovers, is that the man had not drowned. The second thing he discovers, was that the city police had no intention of investigating what was most likely a murder. His investigation takes many turns. It exposes several serious crimes, anyone of which could be the motive for murder. Each crime seems to lead to a legendary hit man known as the Dragon Maker. He has been a legend for twenty years and no one knows his identity.

The Life Of A Horse Trader

This book contains forty years of memories of a horse trainer and horse trader. It is not a biography but ra-

ther snapshots of a life lived among horses and horse-men. It points out the peculiarities of many of these horsemen. Some good some bad, but all interesting. During those forty years I tried to dance every dance and sing every song. I look back on my life and consider it well lived. Every day was an adventure and most of the people I associated with were interesting if nothing else.

Cowboy With A Gun

This story follows a boy from a homesteader's farm in the mountains of Arizona. We watch him as he goes from a homeless kid with an old colt pistol, to a deadly gunman before he is old enough to shave. The story proves that the old saying, that a colt was an equalizer of men, was true. He became better than most with the goal of saving a ranch for a girl he had never met but loved

9 798645 120290